Things used to be pretty calm around Winport Middle School. It was just my best friend Marcia and me and our crazy friend Cap. Marcia and I spent most of our time goofing around with Cap and talking about the major crush I had on David Cruise.

And then came the election for class president. David Cruise asked me to be his campaign manager, and I was thrilled at first. But then I found out his opponent was none other than Cap. To make matters worse, these crazy rumors started going around about Cap–like the one about him hanging around with the town weirdo, the guy every-one calls The Wolfman.

I tried to convince myself that the rumors about Cap weren't true. After all, those rumors could cost him the election! But one dark night on my walk home, I thought I saw them–Cap and The Wolfman together in the darkness. It just had to be my imagination. The rumors couldn't be true, could they?

Middle School Rumors

by Deborah M. Nigro

cover photo by John Strange

Published by Worthington Press
7099 Huntley Road, Worthington, Ohio 43085

Printed in the United States of America

10 9 8 7 6 5 4 3 2 1

ISBN 0-87406-372-8

*To my wonderful parents and sister
Pamela, Alice B. Duffy , and
other good friends.*

One

HIS real name is David Cameron, but everybody calls him "The Captain," or "Cap" for short. Last Christmas he transferred here to Winport Middle School from California and became our unofficial class clown after his hilarious performance in the school musical. Watching his tall, lanky form shooting baskets in the empty gymnasium, I realized that Cap was the only person I'd ever met who actually was born in Hollywood. At times I wondered how he really felt about living here in the suburbs of Boston.

Cap's big dream is to become a professional actor. But he doesn't look like those cute guys you see in the movies. Actually, he's kind of homely. His ears stick out. He wears wire-rimmed glasses perched on his sharp nose, and he's weird—sometimes very weird. A few kids claim that he takes walks at night on Winport Beach with a mysterious character who they call "The Wolfman." The Wolfman, they say, is a strange, old man with a long, white beard and an even stranger pet—a wild dog, or maybe a wolf. Since Cap and I are good friends, I thought he wouldn't mind if I asked him about The Wolfman. But I just couldn't. He'd probably just laugh at me anyway for believing anything so crazy. But I was still curious.

Glancing toward the bleachers, I saw my forgotten gym bag sitting on the highest row of seats. I sighed because I had to pass Cap to climb up and retrieve it, and since I was already late for class, I didn't have time to stop and talk to him. Cap's in most of my classes. I like him a lot, but he teases me and sometimes even embarrasses me. My best friend, Marcia, says it's probably because he's got a crush on me, but I'm not so sure of that. I think he teases me because I can't resist teasing him back.

"Hi, Lori. I've been watching that bag for you," he called out, making a great show of aiming the basketball as I hurried by.

"How'd you know it was mine?" I called back from the top row. "It looks just like everyone else's."

"That's easy. I saw you leave it there after

your gym class today."

"And you let me leave without it? Some friend you are, Cap."

I grumbled as I grasped the handle and made my way back down to the shiny gym floor.

Cap finally took a shot, but missed. "Well, I knew you'd come back for it, so I've been hanging around, waiting."

"Waiting? Why? I thought you'd be at Ms. Bosco's election meeting by now. It'll be starting any minute."

"Oh, I'll get there as soon as Coach Burke finishes with us here. I've been waiting because I wanted to talk to you."

The side door opened, and Coach Burke, along with the rest of the class, trooped noisily into the gym. "Cap, you *know* I'm running for class treasurer, and I can't be late for the meeting. Can we talk later?" I asked.

"Looks like we'll have to," he said as his voice faded a little. He took another shot. This time the ball dropped neatly through the hoop. Grinning broadly, he dribbled the ball toward his teammates at the opposite end of the gym.

"Hey! Nice shot, Cap!" I shouted across the gym. I spotted Marcia waiting for me as I turned around and started walking toward the door. She gestured anxiously for me to hurry. "Listen, I'll see you later, okay?" I yelled as I followed Marcia from the gym.

Marcia grabbed my arm and pulled me in the direction of Ms. Bosco's homeroom. Her blue eyes were wide with excitement. "Where have you been, Lori?" she scolded. "I waited ten minutes for you after science."

"Oh, I left my stupid gym bag on the bleachers. What's going on?"

Marcia lowered her voice. "Listen, I overheard a bunch of kids in the cafeteria talking about David Cruise. He plans to run for class president!"

I rolled my eyes. "Marcia, that's not news. Last year, he was president and did a great job. He got the whole school fired up and working together for the mini-Olympics. I mean it's natural for him to run again, and I'm sure everyone expects him to."

"But wait," she said, waving her hand in front of me, "that's not the best part! Bobby Troup told Susan Levenson that David wants you to be his campaign manager! Of course, he doesn't know that you're running for treasurer and that *I'm* going to be *your* campaign manager."

I stood speechless as Marcia broke into a triumphant smile. "You mean David wants me?" I asked. "Why me?"

"Well, maybe because your mother was elected to the school board, and because you came in second place in last year's essay contest. He probably thinks you know politics and that you're one of the smartest students."

"Are you kidding, Marcia?" I cried, unable to believe my ears. "This is impossible! You know that I've had a crush on David Cruise since sixth grade! Remember how we used to walk by his house at night so we could peek at him through the living room window? That was before he moved to the penthouse. Finally, after two years of trying to get his attention, I gave up."

"Yeah, it's kind of hard to spy on a guy who lives on the 15th floor," Marcia joked, then giggled. "I wonder if he ever found out who was sending him those love notes."

It was my turn to giggle. "I certainly hope not. That was probably the dumbest, most immature thing I ever did."

"Shhh!" she said, tilting her head a little to the right. "Don't look now, but he's over there by the water fountain with Bobby."

I dared to look over at him, and I smiled. To my astonishment, he smiled back—not just a little grin, but a big smile. Would the cutest, most popular boy at Winport Middle

School really ask me to manage his campaign? I followed Marcia into homeroom and practically floated toward the front row of desks. *So, this is how it feels to be on cloud nine,* I thought.

Two

MS. Bosco rose from her chair and clapped her hands to get everyone's attention. "Settle down, people," she said. "I must say I'm very impressed that so many of you are interested in this election. How many were involved last year?"

I raised my hand. David was sitting at the desk across from mine, and his hand also was in the air. We exchanged grins, and Tracey Raines flashed me a smile, too. Tracey was a close friend of David's, and I guess she figured that if David needed me to get elected, she'd better be nice. Before I got carried away, though, I reminded myself that David hadn't asked me to join his campaign yet.

"You're in the eighth grade now," continued Ms. Bosco, "and this year, I believe you're ready to participate in a real campaign.

We're even going to use some of the methods that are used to elect our state and national officials."

The whole class began chattering at once. "You can talk among yourselves later," she broke in, "but right now I want to hear your suggestions for planning the campaign."

"Who needs a campaign? Cruise can't lose!" chanted Bobby Troup.

"Cruise can't lose?" Ms. Bosco mused. "That's pretty good, Bobby," she said. "It's too bad slogans alone don't win elections," she added with a smile. "Now, there are three other offices to consider: vice president, secretary, and treasurer."

"Don't we start with a primary election, Ms. Bosco?" asked Marcia, hesitating a little.

"Right, Marcia. That's very good. Yes, a primary narrows the slate to two candidates for each office. To make our campaign as fair as possible, we'll announce our plans at Friday's assembly. That way, any student that's interested in running for office can place his or her name on the ballot. David, although you're our incumbent president..."

"I'll be glad to make the announcement to the class," he offered, lounging confidently in his seat.

"Normally, that would be your job, David,"

replied Ms. Bosco, "but I think speaking at the assembly would give you unfair publicity. We're going to run this like a real presidential election. So, as a neutral party, I'm going to make the announcement myself."

David didn't reply. Out of the corner of my eye, I saw him blush slightly, his lips twisted in a small scowl.

"Ms. Bosco," I said nervously, "let's photocopy the announcement right away and put one on each homeroom bulletin board. Then everybody will be prepared to ask questions or place their names on the ballot right after the assembly."

"Good idea, Lori," Ms. Bosco said. "It looks like you learned a thing or two during your mother's school board campaign. That's wonderful. Now, are there any other ideas?" she asked as she looked around the room.

"When's the primary, Ms. Bosco?" asked a boy in the back.

"Well, how about two weeks from Tuesday? That would be the traditional day for elections. Then the final election should be three weeks after that, to give the candidates enough time to make their speeches, take polls, and debate the issues."

The classroom door opened, and Cap strolled in. "Did someone say speeches? Now you're talking my language," he said, blushing a little when his eyes met Ms. Bosco's. "Um, sorry I'm late, Ms. Bosco. Coach Burke kept us after class."

"Yeah, are you sure you weren't in detention?" snickered Bobby.

"Not this time," Cap shrugged as he dropped into the seat behind me. He didn't seem to mind the comment.

"That's all right, Cap," said Ms. Bosco. "Someone can fill you in on what we've covered. Now, I'm going to need all of you to fill out these questionnaires. And please be sure to answer the last question: 'What is the biggest issue facing the eighth-grade class this year?' This is especially important. And I'll include your answers in the election announcement." She began passing out the questionnaires. "Now, can anyone tell me the purpose of an election campaign?"

"Winning!" blurted Cap.

Ms. Bosco smiled as the rest of the class began laughing. "Well, Cap, you've certainly got a point. Winning is important. But one of the main reasons for a campaign is to allow the candidate to voice his or her opinion on certain issues. That way, people can make intelligent choices when they cast their ballots."

"Hey, Lori, did I miss anything?" Cap tapped me on the shoulder and whispered.

I turned in my seat and tried to give him a quick summary of the meeting. "You must be excited about running for treasurer, huh?" Cap asked. "Politics are great," he whispered. "It's the next best thing to show biz."

I smiled back at him. "Well, I'll give the treasurer's race my best shot," I said, turning away from him. I glanced over at David and Tracey, who were whispering together. *What should I do if David really asks me to manage his campaign? I have good grades, belong to the gymnastics team and drama club, and have a terrific best friend.*

But David and his friends seemed somehow special. They were known to be part of the "in group," or "cool group," and everyone called them "The Cruise Crowd." They always wore the latest styles and lived in the richest sections of town. Everyone wanted invitations to their parties. I wondered what it would be like to be rich. Marcia and I often imagined what it would be like to go on vacation to Disneyworld, or to go to the mall and spend as much money as we wanted. *Would I really be hanging out with them?*

After the meeting, David cornered me in the hall. Marcia was talking with Cap beside the row of lockers, but I saw that her eyes were on me. I hoped she wouldn't make me crack a smile, so I looked away. "Lori, how would you like to be my campaign manager?" David asked. "You know, a brain like yours could really help me win this election," he said as he leaned on the lockers and tapped his fingers on them.

"Um," I muttered nervously. "Do you really need my help, David? Bobby says that Cruise can't lose," I answered, laughing a bit. It seemed I'd never been so close to him, and I could feel my face starting to blush.

"Aw, ignore Bobby," urged David with a smile, his white teeth gleaming against what was left of his summer tan.

Tracey Raines joined us by the water fountain. "I'll bet you're excited that Davey's asked you to lead his campaign," she said sweetly.

"Well, it is nice of David to ask," I agreed, not knowing what to say, "but I was going to run for class treasurer."

"Oh, come on, Lori, that's a boring job," Tracey said. "All the treasurer does is collect class dues and give reports at student meetings. Trust me, Davey's campaign will be a lot more fun."

"That's right," added David. "There'll be

parties and maybe a big campaign rally. What do you say?"

I was so tempted to say yes, but I didn't. "Let me think about it, David." I wished I could have made a firm decision, but I'd really been looking forward to running for office myself.

Tracey, now waving to her friend, Nicole Rossi, wasn't listening to me. "Nice dress, Nicole!" she shouted and then turned back to me. "We're having a strategy meeting at Rainesworth tomorrow afternoon. You'll come, won't you?" she asked in a bossy tone.

Both Marcia and my family had been looking forward to seeing me run for treasurer. And I'd been thinking about it myself all summer, but, at the same time, I hated to miss the chance to be with the crowd at Rainesworth. Tracey's mansion had once been photographed for a national magazine, and this would be my chance—probably my only chance—to see it.

"I'll be there, Tracey," I blurted out. "Is it okay if Marcia Clancy comes along?"

Tracey's smile faded. "Shouldn't this be a private strategy meeting for the campaigners?"

"Uh, sure. I understand." I tried not to sound too disappointed.

"Great!" David said. "Then we'll see you tomorrow at two o'clock. We're all going to get a hamburger, and I'm starved! See you later!" He disappeared down the stairs, with Tracey at his heels. Suddenly, I felt a little left out and wished they'd asked me along. Then someone tapped me on the shoulder.

I jumped, startled. "Cap, don't scare me like that!" I was feeling a little angry that they had left me out, and I could feel myself snap at him.

"Sorry, Lori. I was only joking. What are you doing–dreaming about your treasurer's race?"

"Well, I've changed my mind about running, Cap." There was a touch of pride in my voice when I added, "David Cruise just asked me to manage his presidential campaign. Doesn't it sound exciting?"

"Too bad you accepted," he said, crossing his arms across his faded Mickey Mouse T-shirt.

"Too bad? Why? What's that supposed to mean?"

"Well, as a math whiz, you'd be a great treasurer. Anyway, hanging out with those guys might be exciting and fun, but how do you really feel about David as a candidate? Are you convinced he'll make the best class president?" Cap asked seriously.

At this point, I was fuming. "Cap Cameron, I wish you'd get off my case!"

"Look, I'm just asking. But," he hesitated, "I'll admit I have an ulterior motive for trying to talk you out of helping Cruise."

"And what would that motive be?"

"Well, my *own* presidential campaign. If you manage Cruise, he'll have the big advantage."

Secretly I was flattered, but I didn't know how to respond. I didn't want to hurt his feelings. "Yeah, but I can't wait to see your special campaign tactics or hear your first speech. What will you do? Give it while you're wearing that Captain Hook costume we made together for last year's musical? Whether you're in the drama club or not, you're always finding some outrageous way to get attention, Cap."

"Hey that costume's not a bad idea," he said, nodding and rubbing his chin. He looked thoughtfully down the hall. "You know," he said, looking back at me, "that Captain Hook character gave me my nickname, and name recognition is really important for politicians. So, are you sure you want to work for Cruise and not for me?"

"Yeah," I said, a little hesitantly. "But if

you're serious about running, Cap, you know I wish you all the luck."

"Thanks, Lori, but don't mention it to anyone yet. I'm not ready to announce it."

"No problem," I said, relieved that he stopped asking me to help with his campaign. "My lips are sealed." I glanced around and saw that no one was around. It's times like these when we were alone that I always wanted to ask him about the Wolfman rumors, but I could never get enough nerve— and I didn't have it now either. "Cap, did you see where Marcia went?"

"Yeah, I think she went to her locker. She said she'd wait for you by the main exit. Hey, I've got to go now. Mom has to get to work, and I have to baby-sit Billy and Jeff."

"Again? That's the third night this week you've had to watch them. I'll bet you're great with them, especially when it comes to telling bedtime stories. Will you have to keep doing this for long?"

"I will if Mom's working late."

"Can your grandmother help out a bit? I've seen how she adores playing with them."

"Oh, she loves them for sure, but I think watching both of them for very long is too much for her to handle. They usually go right to sleep, though, so I can get my homework done. See you, Lori."

I watched Cap hurrying down the long, empty corridor. After his father died a year ago in California, his family had to move back here to live with his grandmother. I wondered how he kept his grades so high with all the responsibility he had at home. I really did respect him—he always seemed to be there when anyone needed him. Then it occurred to me that Cap never said what he wanted to talk with me about earlier in the gym. And I'd forgotten to ask.

Just then, Bobby Troup appeared from the shadowy alcove beside the water fountain. "So, crazy Cap Cameron wants to run for president. If you're smart, Lori, you'll join the Cruise campaign. Together, we can beat Cap and anybody else dumb enough to think he can beat David."

"Listen, I've decided to support David, and I'm as sure as you are that he'll win. But please don't say anything about Cap's campaign. He doesn't want anybody to know he's running until he announces it himself."

"Whatever you say," agreed Bobby.

There was something about him I didn't quite trust. And I was a little angry that he was there, hiding and listening to our conversation. "See you at Rainesworth," I muttered, heading down the hall to find Marcia. How could I tell her my treasurer's race was off? She'd been hard at work helping me make so many campaign plans. I hoped she would understand that I couldn't resist the opportunity to join the Cruise crowd.

Three

"WHAT do you think, Marcia—a little more lip gloss?" I asked, peering at myself in the mirror over the tiny sink in the back room of my mother's Winport Center bookshop.

"What you really need is some mascara," Marcia advised.

"Yeah, but you know my parents won't let me wear eye makeup."

"Neither will mine, but at least get rid of that barrette. It just looks too childish. Just let your hair hang down to your shoulders, and smooth out your bangs." She unsnapped the metallic gold bow that was holding my hair back. "There. Looks good, huh?"

"If only I were blond, like Tracey," I moaned.

"Don't worry about Tracey. David seems to like class and brains, and I'd say you've got both. I've always liked your dark hair anyway."

"That's easy for you to say," I said, tugging one of her orange curls. "Can't miss you in a crowd." Marcia smiled. "You know, I'm glad you understand why I'm dropping the campaign, especially after you did all that work."

"Oh well, who wouldn't want to join the Cruise crowd at Rainesworth?" Marcia said and shrugged. "At first I was a little disappointed that I wouldn't have a campaign to manage. But I'll still be on the ballot committee, right in the middle of the action." Her eyes became wide as she rubbed her hands together and laughed.

My mother poked her head through the red relief curtain that separated the back room from the rest of the shop. "Are you ready, Lori? There's nobody here right now, and it's a good time to close up for a few minutes while I drive you to Rainesworth."

"Sure, I'm all set, Mom."

"Your white dress looks lovely, honey, but I thought you were saving it for the school dance."

"I was, but I wanted to wear something special for Rainesworth."

"Mrs. Stanton, can I mind the shop while

you're gone?" asked Marcia. "I spend a lot of time here, and I know the stock and how to run the cash register. Lori even let me write up a credit card sale last week."

"I guess that'll be all right," Mom agreed after a brief hesitation. "In fact, Marcia, I'll pay you if you'll work for a couple of hours this afternoon. Saturdays are really busy."

"Oh, great! My first job!" said Marcia enthusiastically. She followed us outside and stood on the welcome mat, waving good-bye as we pulled away from the curb. I glanced back at her through the car window, feeling a funny mixture of excitement, guilt, and loneliness. Marcia was my best friend in the world, and I was leaving her behind while I visited the most famous house in Winport.

I'd considered asking Tracey again if I could bring Marcia along to the meeting, but I chickened out. I don't know what Tracey has against Marcia. Maybe it's Marcia's good grades. Or maybe it's the fact that Marcia's parents are divorced, and her mother can't afford to buy her a lot of new clothes. I remember one time when Tracey called her a geek behind her back, and I'm still mad at myself for letting her get away with it.

"Do you wish Marcia was going with you?" Mom asked. Sometimes it's really weird how my mom can read my mind.

"I know she'd love to see Rainesworth," I said, opening my bag to make sure I had the notes and sample posters I'd sketched for the campaign.

"Honey, you know your father and I hoped you'd run for class office yourself," she said, guiding the car around the busy corner by Freedom Market. "Are you sure you want to drop it to help David? You've always rather admired him, haven't you?"

"Mom..."

"Okay, hon, I was just wondering. I know you must be looking forward to getting to know him. But you were so excited about the idea of running, and we thought it would be a great experience for you."

We didn't speak again until we drove through the big iron gates and along the landscaped driveway to Rainesworth. I knew she was right about giving up my campaign, but she was also right that I was excited to work with him. Mom stopped in front of the gray, stone mansion. Parked in the driveway were Tracey's family's cars— a Jaguar and a Mercedes. "Don't be so nervous, Lori," Mom said as I opened the door. "You'll be just fine, and you might even find out that the people who live here aren't much different from everybody else. Go ahead, hon," she said and winked.

"Yeah, but, just look at this place!"

She patted my arm. "Don't forget what I said. Keep your eyes and ears open, and have fun."

"Right, Mom. Bye-bye, and thanks for the ride." I got out and shut the door.

"Phone me if you need a ride home," Mom called out the window as she drove away.

I pushed the doorbell and heard chimes ringing inside the huge house. No answer. Shuffling my feet, I waited a few moments, and then I rang it again. The carved oak door opened, and a woman I guessed to be the maid greeted me. "Good afternoon," she said as she brushed the hair away from her face. She looked tired and very overworked. "Please, come on in. They're in the downstairs playroom, the last door to the right." She pointed vaguely in the direction of a stair-case and walked away, down a long hall.

The living area was the size of a ballroom. It could have been a movie set. My eyes swept over the shimmering, crystal chandelier and the elegant, antique furnishings. Slowly, I crossed the ruby-toned Oriental carpet, glancing at all the oil paintings framed in gold and hung on a wall covered with wallpaper that looked like blue silk. When I reached the door that the maid had pointed out, I turned the brass knob.

Music blasted from the playroom. Then Nicole Rossi, Tracey's best friend, appeared at the bottom of the stairs. She was wearing jeans and a sweatshirt. Actually, they were designer jeans and a Yale University sweatshirt, and I suddenly felt very overdressed. She grinned up at me. "Hi, Lori. Where are you going in that dress? To the prom? Only kidding. I'm on my way up for some more tonic."

"Tonic" is what Bostonians call soft drinks. Nobody knows why. Nicole bounded up the stairs and stopped beside me. I didn't like her crack about my dress, but I ignored it. "I'll have grape soda if you've got it," I asserted, lifting my chin.

"One grape soda," Nicole nodded, stepping through the door and closing it behind her.

I moved downstairs to join the unexpectedly large gang in the playroom. There certainly weren't any campaign strategies being worked on here. There were bowls of popcorn and chips on all the tables, and people were drinking soft drinks as they danced. And they seemed to be dancing everywhere! They were dancing on top of the coffee tables, and on two beige sofas near the back of the room. A video blazed across a five-foot television screen. The shag carpet was littered with crumpled paper plates and crushed corn chips. Everyone was in jeans and sweaters. *Did I look silly all dressed up? Was this really a meeting to plot our campaign strategy, or just an excuse for a party?*

Nicole handed me a grape soda. "Sorry I made that remark about your dress," she said. "It's pretty. I have one just like it." Before I could answer, she ran off to fling her arms around some husky boy I'd never seen before.

I flipped open the top of the soda can, took a sip, and glanced around for someone I knew. Finally I spied Tracey's head of golden hair behind the bar. But David Cruise was no-where to be seen.

"Hey, Lori, what's with the dress?" asked Bobby Troup.

"Well," I said, trying to act confident, "campaigning is serious business. I thought I should dress up."

"Yeah, I agree," Bobby said. "How about dumping that bag and your tonic so we can dance?"

"Sure, okay." There was still something I didn't trust about him, but I thought I better get to know him better. I put my bag on an empty chair and tried to set my drink on a table packed with empty cans, half-filled bowls of potato chips, and crumpled napkins. Just then, someone spilled grape soda onto the suede sofa. I grabbed for a paper napkin, but someone gently pushed me from behind.

"Never mind that, Lori, just get out there and dance," yelled Tracey from a few steps away. "Grace, our maid, will clean that up." *Poor Grace*, I thought, making my way into the crowd of dancers with Bobby. *Imagine having to clean up after a party like this?*

"Bobby, who are these kids?" I asked as we started to dance.

"Their parents belong to North Shore Yacht Club, like Davey, Tracey, Nicole, and me. I'll introduce you to a few of them."

"So, where are Mr. and Mrs. Raines?"

"Oh, they're in New York. Sometimes Tracey stays here alone with the maid. That's probably why this is such a dynamite party: no parents!"

"Sure...right," I mumbled. Mom and Dad wouldn't be pleased if they knew there were no adults supervising the party, and it didn't look like Grace was setting down any rules. But I didn't want to sound like a baby. Besides, I know I can handle myself pretty well. I mean I'm smart enough to say no to beer or drugs. I was glad there wasn't anything like that here.

"Just wait until our candidate finds out what a great dancer you are, Lori," Bobby said, smiling. I glanced around the room to see how everyone else was dancing.

I felt myself blushing at the compliment. "Oh, thanks, Bobby. You're not bad yourself." He smiled and looked down at his feet. It was the first time I'd seen him look shy. Then I paused, "So, where's David? Is he here yet?"

"I think he and his father are out somewhere buying a new sailboat. Wait a minute, here comes our man now. Hey, Dave! Hey, over here!"

David waved and smiled from where he stood on the bottom step of the staircase. "Hi, guys. Having fun?" he shouted over the music.

He moved toward us, but it didn't take long before he was trapped—surrounded with people. "Hey, everybody, it's David Cruise!"

"Hey, Dave, my man, you finally made it," bellowed Bobby.

"David, you're finally heeere!" yelled Tracey.

Bobby said a fast good-bye and took off

to join the kids gathered around our candidate. With all the cheering going on, it looked like David had just won the whole election. It was then that I noticed Bobby was wearing gray cords and a green sweater almost exactly like David's. I remember last year when he used to wear his brown hair kind of long, but now it was cut short, just like David's. Funny.

"Hi, there. I'm Ted, Tracey's cousin. Would you like to dance?" asked a nervous-looking blond boy in a red shirt.

What I really wanted to do was get started on the strategy meeting, but there wasn't much hope of that with the party in full swing. "I'm Lori, um, a friend of Tracey's," I answered. "And, yeah, I'd like to dance."

It was a good hour before I could pry David loose from the crowd, but it gave me a chance to dance a little more and meet a few more people. Some of them went to private schools, and a few of them had even traveled all over the world—to Mexico, to Europe, and even to Australia. The guys bragged about the new cars they'd be driving once they got their learner's permits. It seemed like practically all of them wore designer jeans, expensive running shoes, and brand-name everything else.

They did the kinds of things Marcia and I

only dreamed about doing. I couldn't wait to call her and tell her all about it when I got home.

I was sipping my second can of tonic when a voice called out, "Listen, everybody. Meet my new campaign manager, Lori Stanton."

"Huh?" My head shot up to see David balancing on a bar stool, pointing right at me.

"Way to go, Lori!" someone yelled.

"Hey, hey, hey!" hollered another.

"Cruise can't lose with Lori!" bellowed Bobby.

David pushed through the crowd, grasped my hand, and held it high in the air. The pounding music couldn't drown out the burst of applause. My face went hot with nervous excitement. You'd think I was the guest of honor. "Hey, let's look at those campaign plans, okay?" David smiled.

"They're in my bag on that chair. Uh...someone's sitting on it." I said, a little worried. I imagined all of my hard work—all of my notes and posters—getting smashed and wrinkled.

"Get off that bag, Belmont!" David called to the heavyset boy who was squashing my tote bag. With a sheepish grin and a whispered apology, he got up and handed the bag to David, and the two boys exchanged playful punches. Then David smiled and handed me the bag as he escorted me upstairs to the peacefulness of the living room.

He motioned for me to sit with him on a beautiful, antique love seat covered in gray velvet. Nervously, I got out my folder of notes and sketches from the bag. I held my breath while David reviewed them. "You know, this is a really good first draft for my primary speech," he said. "And I like the part about my being the best candidate for all the students." Quickly, he flipped through the poster sketches. "These are pretty good, Lori, but my dad's already made up some designs on the drawing board at his printing plant. Real professional stuff. Should be a big help to me, er, us..."

"Sorry, you two, but mother doesn't allow anyone to sit on those chairs."

I jumped up at the sound of Tracey's voice, but David remained where he was. "C'mon, Trace, you're sounding like my father. Besides, we're having a conference. Remember that campaign meeting, Trace?" he asked a little sarcastically.

"Yes, very funny, David. Well, sorry about the big crowd. I really did only invite five or six kids from the yacht club, but then they brought their friends. I guess things got slightly out of hand."

The telephone rang. Tracey walked over to a small circular table and picked up a small, sleek telephone that was behind a huge vase of fresh red roses. "It's for you, Davey. It's your father. He said he's going to pick you up in 15 minutes, and he wants you to please be ready."

"Tell him that's fine, will you, Trace? Hey Lori, do you want a lift home?"

I saw Tracey's face fall when I nodded yes. She stuck with us like some kind of chaperon all the way down the hallway. I knew she had a crush on him. Then the car horn blew. I must admit, I felt proud to think she might be jealous of me.

David's father was a big man with a booming voice. I felt like a movie star as I stepped inside his silver Mercedes. I sat back in the soft, leather seat and buckled my seat belt. He and David were pretty quiet most of the way. They dropped me off at the bookshop. Looking past the window display, I could see Mom smiling. It looked like she was talking with someone. I crossed the street and opened the door.

"What's going on here?" I asked, and then I grinned as two angelic, baby faces looked up at me from a double-seated stroller.

"Where's your big brother? Huh, boys?" I asked as I lightly patted each tiny head.

"Cap's looking at the theater books, as usual," said Mom.

"Here I am, Lori," Cap said, as he popped out from behind the nonfiction shelf. He quickly walked toward me as he pushed his glasses up on his nose. "Hey, I saw you getting out of Mr. Cruise's flashy car, and you're all dolled up in your fancy dress, too. So what's the story? Is Rainesworth all it's cracked up to be?"

"You bet, and more. Cap, that house is absolutely incredible." Just then I felt a gentle tugging on me. "Hey, there, little one. You stop pulling on my skirt." I laughed and knelt down to tweak the baby's button nose. "Which twin is he, Cap?"

"That's Billy. And watch out for Jeff. They just finished my banana, and Jeff has a tendency to be the sloppier one.

Smaller and paler than Billy, Jeff held out his chubby arms to me. Cap wasn't kidding. Every finger was sticky. But I couldn't resist lifting him out of the stroller. I sat down on the floor of the shop and snuggled him in my lap. *A little banana won't hurt my dress*, I thought. "Sticky hands, or no sticky hands, you're a sweetheart," I cooed.

Cap dropped down beside me, holding open a picture book about famous Broadway musicals. "Just look at these costumes!" he cried, showing me a color photograph of the cast of a play.

"Oh, aren't these neat!" I agreed. "Boy, imagine being able to wear stuff like that, Cap. The drama club would never be the same." He nodded and smiled. I looked down at baby Jeff. His little eyes could barely stay open. "What's the matter, baby? Have I bored you to pieces already?"

"Don't worry, Lori, he does that sometimes. Suddenly he just conks out, sound asleep. All of us are hoping he's going to be okay. Mom says the doctors think he has a heart condition that'll need surgery. Somehow I just know he's going to be all right."

My heart sank. I put my arms around Jeff, wishing I could do something. "Cap, I'm so sorry. I didn't know that. You never mentioned it." I looked around for Mom, but she'd gone into the back room.

"Well, what's the point of talking about it? It won't change the situation," Cap said, looking down at the floor.

I looked up at him and realized that for the first time since I'd known him, his ever-smiling face was veiled in sadness.

Four

O N Monday morning, the whole classroom was filled with talk about the election. Marcia and I decided to go out and see if Ms. Bosco had posted the announcement on the bulletin board. "It looks like our top campaign issue is how to spend the money that was raised for the middle school by the Parents' Council," I commented.

"So, what's Cruise's stand on the issue?"

"Well, he said that he wants to buy new uniforms and new equipment for the sports teams. But, to tell you the truth, there was so much happening at Rainesworth that we didn't end up making much progress on the campaign. It got kind of wild."

"Boy, I wish I'd been there," Marcia said, "but you know I really had a good time working with your mother at the bookstore."

"Yeah, well, you know how much she likes you, and Mom said you were great with the customers."

"Oh yeah? Hmm. And she was really generous. It was great getting paid. Listen, Lori," she continued eagerly, "would you ask Tracey to let me come along the next time you meet at Rainesworth?"

"Well," I hesitated, not knowing what to say. "I'm not sure where our next meeting will be." I knew I couldn't promise Marcia that I'd ask Tracey to let her come to a meeting. Tracey might say no, and Marcia's feelings would be hurt.

Then, to my relief, she changed the subject. "By the way, did you hear that Gail Trent is running for president?"

"You heard right," broke in Gail. She was a tall, athletic girl with pretty, short hair. Gail always seemed to be in motion. "Our marching band is the best in the state, and we deserve a chance to prove it," she said with conviction. "I think the money raised by the Parents' Council should be used to send the Vikettes to the regional championships in Springfield."

"Hmm. That sounds pretty good," said Marcia. "Gail, do you know who else is running?"

I knew, of course, but I had promised Cap that I'd keep quiet about his candidacy. But, as it turned out, I might as well have broadcast it to the whole school. Thanks to Bobby Troup, Cap's presidential hopes were common knowledge by Friday's assembly.

* * * * *

On Friday, Ms. Bosco had a special table set up in back of the auditorium. Bobby and I were watching as the candidates signed up. "Can you believe that freak Cameron thinks he can beat Cruise?" Bobby said.

"Cap's not a freak. He's just different."

"I'll say he's different! Any guy who hangs a 'Save The Whales' banner from the TV antenna on the school roof is definitely different. I still haven't figured out how he got up there. What's so funny, Lori?"

"Remember the crowd he attracted? And the principal's face when he gave Cap five hours of detention? Poor Mr. Riley was trying to look serious, but he kept cracking up with laughter just like the rest of us."

"Come on, Lori. He made the school look ridiculous. Every newspaper in Boston ran a picture of it."

"Well," I said, defending him, "when he believes in a cause, he certainly knows how to attract publicity for it."

"I still wonder a little if a guy who hangs

out with The Wolfman should be class president. You have to admit it's pretty weird."

"Yeah, but we don't really know if that's all true. I mean, it's possible that they're only rumors," I said firmly. *Sooner or later*, I thought to myself, *I'd like to clear up this Wolfman thing*.

"Bobby, you're too smart to believe in wolfmen. Besides, my mother always says, 'No candidate has it made.' David should campaign hard, or somebody else could win."

"You're the boss," Bobby responded.

"Bobby, look. Of course I want David to win, but I also want to run a fair campaign. I hope Cap Cameron doesn't think *I* told everybody he was running."

Bobby placed his hand over his heart, and spoke in a soft, high-pitched voice, "Lori, if you think I told anybody..."

"Come on, I don't *think* you told anybody, Bobby. I *know* you did," I said, getting a little angry.

Just then David walked by. "Hey, guys, how about a strategy meeting at Tracey's right after school?" he asked, clapping Bobby on the shoulder. Then he looked at me and winked. "No party this time, Lori. I promise." He held up his hand as if taking an oath.

Tracey came up behind David. "Hey, I

heard that. Okay, Davey, no party, but let's play the new CD my dad bought me in New York. I know you'll like it."

I didn't expect us to get much accomplished at Rainesworth. As it turned out, though, there were only five of us this time, and, except for the music playing in the background, the house was relatively quiet. I loved being at Rainesworth again. Grace, the maid, had done her job well. Not a trace of Saturday's wild party remained. I suggested assignments while everyone snacked from a tray on the coffee table.

"Naturally, David, you'll go around talking to people between classes, at gym, and in the cafeteria. Discuss your views with anybody who'll listen."

"Don't you mean anybody who's anybody?" Tracey interrupted. They all laughed.

"Look, everybody," I said with hesitation, "no matter how popular you are, you only get one vote. That's how the system works. So, it's important to try to represent every student. That's how you get elected."

"Don't mind us, Lori. We understand," said Nicole, reaching toward the tray. "Here, have one of these."

"Well, now that we know what Cruise will be doing, what are your plans for the rest of us?" asked Bobby. "Did I tell you that I got that attendance list from Ms. Bosco? It gives the names of every member of the eighth-grade class."

I quickly swallowed a bite of the cookie. "Bobby, that's brilliant!" I shouted. "Now each of you can get the students' opinions on the issues and write them down. We can take a poll at the same time, too. Ask everybody who they plan to vote for. You know, Cruise, Cameron, Trent, or undecided?"

"Undecided? Who's he?" giggled Tracey.

Bobby spoke up. "You know, I think Lori's doing a pretty good job. She's got lots of notes here for your primary speech."

"Oh, no," groaned David. "Speeches aren't my thing."

"No way, Cruise! Your speech at our final assembly last June was awesome!" Bobby insisted.

"Well, I like giving them, not writing them," David groaned, grabbing a handful of corn chips. He moved closer to me on the suede sofa. "Let's see what you've got there, Lori," he said.

As usual, my heart started hammering, and my voice sounded a little breathless. It seemed that no matter how much time I spent with David, I was always nervous. "I've got most of the speech written, so don't worry about anything. It would be more effective, though, if you go over these notes later and put the words together in your own way. You know, it would just sound more natural," I explained.

"That's just what I told him last year, when I worked on his campaign speech," nodded Bobby proudly.

David picked up the legal pad and began skimming the first page. "You've made all the important points here. You mentioned my work on last year's mini-Olympics right at the beginning. That's perfect," he said, smiling.

"Well, I thought you should end with your views on the Parents' Council issue," I said, flipping the yellow lined pages. "Here it is."

David scanned the last page. "That's right. I really do think new sports equipment will encourage more kids to participate," he said. "Remind me to take these notes home with me, okay?" He looked up from the paper. "Hey, Trace, how about rerunning that video?" he said as he got up and moved toward the VCR.

"And, turn it up loud so we can dance!" Tracey called out.

"Speaking of dancing, I've got a surprise," grinned David, touching the buttons on the

VCR. "Dad's renting a white limo to take us to the school dance. You too, Lori."

"Oh, wow, we'll look just like the rock stars!" squealed Tracey.

"That's neat. I'd love it," I said, forgetting about the meeting and picturing myself stepping out of the limousine with half the school watching.

Only Bobby continued studying the campaign plans. The strategy meeting was over almost before it had begun.

* * * * *

In health class, Cap and I sit together, and it's the only place he usually doesn't embarrass me. Cap takes health class seriously, unlike Tracey, who pretends to know it all, or Bobby, who constantly giggles during the entire class. Today, though, the only topic on anybody's mind was the primary speeches to be given on Friday.

"Lori, I think the Cruise campaign wins the first round for having the best posters," Cap whispered across the aisle. Mrs. Dale was plugging in the projector for a film we were about to watch.

"But, Cap, we haven't started to make our posters."

"Then what are those huge posters that Cruise, Troup, and some others were hanging in the cafeteria just now?"

"Beats me," I answered, completely bewildered.

"Lori and David, be quiet, please!"

After class, I dashed down to the cafeteria, and, sure enough, there they were. Bobby was climbing down from a stepladder when I walked in. "Are these posters something, or what!" he shouted. David and the other guy, who turned out to be Mr. Cruise, were carrying more of the posters under their arms.

Mr. Cruise removed a tack from between his lips and began hammering up yet another enormous poster.

"Oh, hello, Lori. Nice to see you again."

"Hi. It's nice to see you too. Boy these are great posters, Mr. Cruise."

"Well, thank you, Lori. And I've been quite impressed by your speech writing. It's very good. And here I've saved you the trouble of painting my son's campaign posters by hand. I put these together at work. And how about these color photos of David and that fluorescent-green lettering? With a mug like that, you can't lose. Right, David?" Mr. Cruise boasted, and I noticed David blushing a little and looking uncomfortable. " 'Cruise Can't Lose.' That's a catchy phrase you've coined, son."

"Actually, Dad, Bobby came up with that one."

"Great. Listen, I've got to get back to the office, kids. I know you'll help David to get elected again this year. He's a born winner. See you tonight, Pres."

I was so overwhelmed by the posters that I couldn't think of anything to say. "I told Dad about your sketches, Lori. He liked your original idea," David explained. "The only thing different about these is the photograph." I knew he was trying to make me feel better.

My eyes went to Gail Trent's posters. They were drawings in black, red, and gold colors, and they pictured her in a red Vikettes uniform. But they were clearly overshadowed by David's professionally-printed posters. Suddenly, I just felt like crying. I knew how much time Gail had probably spent on her posters. David's campaign finances were more than just a cut above the rest. And though I knew he wasn't playing unfairly, the whole thing just didn't feel right.

"Wonderful posters," I managed to say. "And they do look like the ones I drew."

David's elaborate posters were unfair to the other candidates' efforts, but it was too late to do anything about them. Anyway, I doubted that the Cruise crowd would agree with me.

Five

TRACEY, Nicole, and Bobby outdid themselves with David's primary poll. They collected opinions from every member of the eighth-grade class. I suspected that many of them were flattered by the attention from the popular kids. The boys especially flipped for Tracey and Nicole. The bottom line was that David was popular even before he became a candidate, so it wasn't a surprise that he had such a big lead.

Gail was doing pretty well, too, but she had the band behind her. Cap didn't have posters or a campaign staff, except for Eddie Waters, his buddy on the basketball team. In fact, Cap wasn't doing much except talking with individuals or small groups about the future of our school. Mom says that kind of quiet campaign can sometimes have excellent results, but I didn't think he could possibly overcome David's lead, or even Gail's.

I was so nervous on the day of David's primary speech that I spilled orange juice all over the front of my blouse and had to change it. Then, after walking two whole blocks in the rain toward school, I realized I'd forgotten my tote bag. By the time I ran back for it and headed to school again, I was late. Rain was coming down in buckets. I broke into a trot, knowing that Marcia would be waiting for me in our usual place at Dom's Delicatessen. Dom was a wonderful, old guy with sparkling, green eyes. He'd always tell Marcia and me jokes when we stopped there to take temporary shelter from the rain.

"Lori, do you want a ride to school?" called out a voice. It was David, waving out the window of his father's Mercedes as it splashed to the curb.

"Thanks, David, but I'm meeting Marcia Clancy at the deli."

"That's okay, Lori. We can pick up your friend, too," blurted Mr. Cruise. "You don't want to be late today."

I didn't need any more persuasion. My hair was dripping, and if I kept on walking, I knew I'd definitely be late. I opened the back door of the sleek sedan and jumped in. Mr. Cruise drove to the deli, but there was no sign of

Marcia. She might have gone into another store to wait for me, but since I couldn't see her in the doorway, I didn't say anything. David was anxious to get to school, and I didn't want to be the one responsible if he arrived late. Maybe Marcia had gone on without me.

When I got to school I raced into homeroom, barely beating the final bell. Marcia wasn't in her seat. I felt terrible. I imagined her still there, waiting for me.

"Listen up, everyone. I'm going to take attendance," said Mr. Poole, our homeroom teacher.

I looked anxiously at the door in the back of the room. So here it was 7:30. The bell had rung. Mr. Poole was about to take attendance, and Marcia Clancy was late. That meant an automatic detention, and it was all my fault.

Mr. Poole began reading the names. "Addison..."

"Here."

"Bernstein..."

"Here."

"Carlson..."

"Here."

"Clancy..."

Just then, the front door opened, and the

principal peeked in. "Excuse me, Mr. Poole. May I have a word with you?"

"I'll be right there, Mr. Riley," said Mr. Poole.

A couple of minutes later, the door in the back of the room opened, and Marcia scurried in. You could tell she'd been running. She was panting. Her face was red, and her hair was wet and glued to her forehead. She shot me a confused, hurt expression, and slid into her seat seconds before Mr. Poole returned to the room.

"Okay, where were we?" he asked, looking down at the attendance sheet on his desk. "Er, Carlson, are you here?"

"Here, Mr. Poole."

"Clancy..."

"Here."

"Davenport..."

"Here."

I let out a big sigh of relief. Marcia was off the hook.

But that wasn't the end of it. After class I tried to catch her to apologize, but she took off the minute we left homeroom. At lunch I sat with the Cruise crowd to go over some last-minute campaign details. I didn't see Marcia until lunch was nearly over. She was sitting at a rear table with some girls from our gymnastics club. I waved, but she didn't see me. Maybe she only pretended she didn't see me.

At last it was time for the speeches to begin. When Tracey, Nicole, and I passed Marcia on our way into the auditorium, she ignored my wave. Her snub hurt me, but I had to force it to the back of my mind when my candidate took the podium.

David delivered his speech just as I'd written it. There was a loud applause and lots of whistles when he finished. I felt proud. I thought about how much fun it would have been to write my own speech for treasurer. *But why think about that now?* I said to myself. Gail followed with a solid plea for class unity and the chance to take the band to Springfield.

Then came Cap, wearing a skirt.

The audience roared! It took the principal, Ms. Bosco, and two other teachers to quiet down everybody. Cap stood patiently with his arms folded, beaming a bit, and waiting for his chance to speak.

"Thank you, Mr. Riley, teachers, and fellow students for giving me this opportunity to run for class president," he began, still smiling. "My unusual outfit has only one purpose. I want to show that my candidacy

57

stands for all of us—guys and girls—who care about our school and our futures. Girls don't lose their femininity if they dress in pants, and guys are still masculine if they choose to wear skirts. After all, soldiers and policemen in Scotland, Greece, and many other countries wear skirts." Cap glanced down at the green-plaid kilt he was wearing over his jeans and running shoes. "Let's ignore labels. Focus on the issues that bring us together, not the ones that drive us apart. About the money raised by the Parents' Council, I think it should be spent on a new computer system. This would help every student learn the skills that are necessary for success in high school, college, and adult life."

His brief speech got a standing ovation. Maybe a few kids were sneering, but Cap had made the boldest move I'd ever seen. And it worked. The Cruise campaign may have won the first round with their posters, but round two definitely belonged to Cap Cameron.

* * * * *

It was Tuesday, the day of the primary. Ms. Bosco's homeroom was packed with candidates and supporters as the ballot committee totaled the final count. While Jack Wong sorted the ballots into marked shoe boxes, Pauline Beazer kept count. "In the race for president, Cruise has 33...34 votes. In the treasurer's race, there are 29 for O'Neill," she called. Marcia was transferring the count to the blackboard with her usual speed and accuracy. I kept watching Kelly O'Neill, who seemed to be way ahead in the treasurer's race. She was grinning from ear to ear. I was a little envious. I kept wondering if I could've beaten her if I'd run.

David appeared beside me. "What's with Cameron's sudden jump, Lori?" he frowned. "Our poll showed me in first place by a mile."

"Don't sweat it, David," I said. "You've got a comfortable lead. Cap's skirt tactic just threw us off temporarily."

"You know, Lori, I'm worried about the way this campaign is developing," David interrupted.

"Why? Because Cap's teammates wore skirts to school today to show their support for him?"

"Waters, Fishman, Smith, and the other guys might look dumb in those skirts, but they sure are attracting a lot of attention!"

"Yeah, look at them up there teasing Ms. Bosco," I sputtered. "You've got to admit that

Eddie looks sort of cute in that little pink number!"

"Cute? Lori, you're supposed to be my campaign manager! While you're giggling over those turkeys, I'm being ignored!"

"Ignored? You are not! Here come Tracey, Bobby, and Nicole. Look, don't worry about it, David. Anyway, would you have worn a skirt to give your speech?"

"Uh, no," he said.

"Of course not. It's not your style. Forget Cap's campaign tactics. You've got to do it your own way—be yourself. Remind people of your involvement in last year's mini-Olympics. It made a real contribution to the school, and keep talking about your plan to help the sports teams. I know plenty of kids who support that."

"Hey, David, great show at the polls!" greeted Bobby. Tracey and Nicole each gave David a dazzling smile.

"That's a big lead you've got there, Davey," Tracey said. "It was your fabulous speech that got them."

You mean my fabulous speech, Tracey, I thought to myself. *Maybe, just maybe, I should have stayed in the treasurer's race!*

Tuning out the Cruise crowd, I glanced through the sea of heads at Marcia. She was sitting in the back of the room, staring thoughtfully out the window. I'd telephoned her house a couple of times, but she'd refused to talk with me. I wanted to apologize for leaving her waiting in the rain. I couldn't stand her being upset with me.

A loud cheer brought me back to earth. "Okay, here we go, people—the final count," said Ms. Bosco. "For the office of secretary, John Pappas goes against Lee Taylor. For treasurer, Kelly O'Neill is up against Joe Hart. Maria Martinez and Frank Dolan are competing for vice president. And now, for president..."

"Drum roll!" called Bobby through cupped hands.

More cheers. Cap, who'd just come in wearing his notorious plaid skirt, stood with Gail Trent.

Laughing, Ms. Bosco concluded, "For president, the winners are Cameron and Cruise!"

Cap placed his arm shyly around a disappointed Gail. "Ms. Bosco, maybe we should have a recount," he said. "There are only five votes between Gail and me, so there might have been a mistake. We want things to be fair, don't we?"

"Certainly, Cap. I'm sure the class

appreciates your gesture. Jack, Pauline, and Marcia, please recount the ballots."

"A recount? Why blow his own chances?" muttered Bobby. "I still say Cameron's nuts."

"Cap does things his way," I defended.

Bobby moved his lips close to my ear. "Believe me, Lori, Cameron is crazy. Maybe worse than crazy. Do you know who I saw him with last Thursday night?"

"No, who?"

"The Wolfman."

Six

"OKAY, Lori. I accept your apology. I know the weather was rotten on primary-speech day, and you didn't want to be late," Marcia said as we walked along the hall. I had finally gotten enough nerve to corner her one evening after gymnastics practice. "But I've got to tell you, I was pretty mad when I saw you in David's car," she said, her voice shaking a little.

"Marcia, I really did look for you in the doorway!"

"I know," she went on. "It's just that things seem different between us lately. Sometimes I wish you hadn't gotten involved with the Cruise crowd."

"You were all for it."

"Yeah, that was before I realized that you'd forget your best friend."

"Marcia, that isn't true," I sighed. "The

campaign takes up a lot of my free time, but it'll be over soon. I'm sorry, I really am." I felt terrible that I had hurt her feelings.

"I know the campaign's fun, but it doesn't leave much time for anything else," Marcia said in a more sympathetic tone. "We've hardly talked about the school dance. Are we still planning to go together, like last year?" Marcia asked. "Unless, of course," she paused, "you have finally landed a date with darling David."

"No, I'm not going with David. My mom will drive you and me to the dance together, just like we planned. Okay?" It felt good to be talking to Marcia again.

"Yeah, that's great," Marcia said with a big grin. "Like you, I couldn't get a date. I think Brian Reynolds only has eyes for his pocket calculator."

We both laughed. I couldn't refuse to attend the dance with my best friend. *Goodbye, limousine,* I thought sadly. I wouldn't be arriving at the dance with the Cruise crowd after all. But Marcia was smiling, and we were friends again. That was a lot more important than a short ride in a limousine. I was feeling much better.

"No offense, Lori, but you look kind of pooped," Marcia commented. "There are bags under your eyes."

"Well, I guess between my homework and the campaign stuff, I'm not getting much sleep," I confessed. "Ever since Cap won the primary recount, David's lost some of his confidence in me. He doesn't agree with Cap's plan about the computers."

"I think it's a great idea. And it wasn't only the skirts that influenced us voters."

"*Us* voters? You mean that Marcia Clancy, my very best friend, voted for the opposing candidate?"

Marcia turned fiery red. I guess she was embarrassed.

"Marcia, you don't have to tell anyone who you voted for," I said, pushing open the school's main door. "Wow, look at it out there. It's getting dark and foggy. Do you want to walk home, or should I call my mother for a ride?"

Marcia shifted her gym bag to her other hand. "Oh, let's walk. We'll pretend we're in the movies. Sherlock Holmes or something." She giggled a little.

The old streets of Winport always become narrower, darker, and gloomier as you get closer to the beach—especially at night. Fog usually gathers quickly, hiding the view of Boston's glittering skyline. Tonight we could hear a ship's bell clang mournfully in the distance. The full moon was like a fuzzy, pale ball that became dimmer in the thickening mist.

Walking along Seawall Drive in the fog and silence, I began to feel kind of spooked. My mind drifted to the strange conversation I'd had with Bobby Troup about Cap and The Wolfman.

"Lori, have you ever seen The Wolfman?" Marcia asked suddenly. I jumped a bit and almost dropped my bag.

"Boy, that's weird, Marcia. I was just thinking about that," I said as I glanced cautiously down the beach. "Do you know Louie Mello in my history class? Well, he said that one night last summei he saw The Wolfman and that strange pet of his right here along the sea wall! When he tried to get closer for a better look, the old man tugged his long beard. He said it was like he made a signal to the animal." Just then I heard a cry. I could make out two white figures moving in the distance. *Gulls. Just sea gulls,* I said to myself. But I quickened my pace. I wondered if Marcia was getting scared.

"So what kind of animal did you say it was?" Marcia asked.

"Like a wolf on a leash, Louie said. Anyway, the animal snapped and snarled. I guess it really scared poor Louie."

Suddenly, it seemed that the warm sea air had turned cold. "They say The Wolfman lives in the old Sturgis place," I said to Marcia as I glared at the dark hill that overlooks the bay. A faint light shone from a single window of the deserted mansion.

"Where else would a Wolfman live?" Marcia whispered, shivering. "The Sturgis mansion is haunted. Let's go, Lori. This discussion's giving me the creeps."

"Yeah, your dad would say that we're missing a microchip if we believe these silly stories," I said, forcing a laugh.

A few yards away, a car appeared from a side street. The headlights formed milky-white triangles in the fog. Gliding toward us, the car hesitated briefly. We both froze. Its lights shone on a bearded man, a boy, and a large animal standing together by the sea wall. A lonely, menacing howl cut the still air. Moving onto Seawall Drive, the high beams of the car blinded Marcia and me as it sped past us into the night.

"Lori, did you see them? The Wolfman and his wolf were standing right beside the wall!"

"And...and the boy standing with them was Cap!" I gasped. "Oh, no, Marcia! Everything

Bobby said about Cap and The Wolfman was true!" I blinked hard, trying to readjust my eyes to the darkness. There was nothing to see but the wall and the fog. The three ghostly figures had vanished.

"So Bobby saw Cap and The Wolfman, too? I know he kids around a lot, but he wouldn't lie, would he? Let's just get out of here!" Marcia squealed.

"Boy, I'm with you. Wait. We can't run away yet. They probably crossed the street and went behind those bushes leading up to the Sturgis place. We didn't see them go because the car lights were in our eyes." Then I paused. "Do you think we should follow them?"

"Follow them? Why?" cried Marcia.

"Well, I'd like to know what's going on. Bobby said he saw Cap with The Wolfman last Thursday night. It's just so strange."

"Well, this Thursday night, Marcia Clancy would like to get home in one piece." She clutched my arm, but when she spoke again her voice was calmer. "Wait a minute, Lori. You know how Cap gets an early dismissal slip from the principal's office almost every Thursday afternoon? That's very mysterious. Do you think it has any connection to The Wolfman?"

"Good thinking, Marcia. I guess there's only one way to find out," I asserted as I started to cross the street. "Come on, Marcia. Where's that spirit of adventure that I know and love?"

Marcia didn't let me down. Together, we mounted the stone steps that cut into the hill leading up to the Sturgis mansion. The thick, untrimmed bushes that surround the house made it difficult to see anything at all. As I looked behind me, a great cloud moved across the moon. Now everything grew darker. The steep steps were damp and slippery. Suddenly, something grabbed part of my hair.

"Oh!" I shouted.

"What is it?" Marcia asked, her voice shrieking. I took a deep breath and reached out with my hand. I touched something sharp and drew back.

"Ah!" I shouted again.

"Lori, what is it? Are you okay?" Marcia asked. Then I realized it was nothing but a thorny twig. I reached over again and unhooked myself.

"Ouch. Sorry, Marcia. Just a twig. I guess this place is starting to get to me."

"Yeah, me too. Look, Lori, I'm getting scared," Marcia whimpered. "Are you really going right up to that porch?"

"Yes. Don't worry. Shhh! Look! There's a lamp in the window. I only want to peek inside."

"Only a peek, she says! You're nuts, Lori."

"Well I figure if Cap's not scared of The Wolfman, or the wolf, then neither am I," I whispered. I sounded much braver than I felt. "Yow!" I stumbled on a loose stone. As frightened as she was, Marcia managed to catch me and keep me from falling.

"Are you okay, Lori?" asked Marcia.

"Yes, I think so. Thanks."

"That porch looks like a cave, complete with bats," Marcia hissed. "There is no way I'm going up to that house!"

"Bats, shmats. Here, hold my gym bag."

"Lori, no!" cried Marcia.

But I didn't listen to her. Quietly, I crept up the broad, wooden stairs as Marcia watched me from a safe distance away from the house. Reaching the top, I looked back over my shoulder for Marcia. She was practically invisible. On tiptoe, I moved toward the door. But then I heard the click of an animal's claws against the bare wood of the porch. I froze. Whatever it was let out a low, angry growl.

I remember hearing that dogs were more likely to attack if they sensed you were afraid.

I wondered if the same applied to wolves. Turning very slowly toward the growl, I said in a high voice, "Good wolfy. Aren't you a pretty boy, er, girl."

I heard a soft whine, and then a cold, wet nose nuzzled my bare knee. *So, wolves are actually friendly,* I thought. I began to breathe once more.

The wolf sat on its haunches, its tail wagging. It had a gentle face with big, black eyes and a long, pointed nose. Its white belly was barely visible, and its tail slapped rhythmically against the porch as it wagged. I put my hand out, and it licked my palm. Then I patted its shaggy head. I took a step to the side to peer into the window.

Cap was seated on a large, leather easy chair. Beside him was a large stone fireplace with a small fire burning in it. The flames made the room flicker in orange and yellow, and in the light I could see Cap's face. He wore the same expression as when he talked about his little brother, Jeff. Behind a rather cluttered desk sat the bearded man. He didn't look mean or spooky at all. In fact, he looked quite friendly. He leaned forward in the soft light, his gray-bearded chin resting on his hand. He looked like he was listening very intently to whatever Cap was saying.

Puzzled, I backed away. I was about to retrace my steps when a shining brass sign on the door caught my attention. After I made out the words, my heart started pounding all over again. It read:

Dr. Samuel Fisher, Psychologist
17 Seawall Drive.

* * * * *

Marcia insisted on knowing every detail of what I saw through The Wolfman's window, but I left out the part about the sign on the door. "He's a peculiar, old guy with a big dog. That's all," I said. "Maybe he's a friend of Cap's grandmother." I couldn't bring myself to tell her that Cap was seeing a psychologist. I didn't know what to make of the whole thing.

"Boy, Lori, wait until we tell the kids at school that we actually followed The Wolfman up to the Sturgis mansion," Marcia replied with a laugh.

"As long as we keep Cap's name out of it," I said. "That's important. It's not fair to him to start any more ridiculous rumors."

I knew Marcia would keep quiet about Cap. Still, I wondered how much longer Cap could keep his meetings with Dr. Fisher a secret.

Seven

I had one whole week to tell David that I couldn't go to the dance with him and his friends. But each day, I couldn't get up enough nerve. Finally, at the last minute, I telephoned him at home. I felt a little foolish explaining that I'd made plans with Marcia long before I joined his campaign. He seemed to understand. At least, I thought he did. After I hung up, I had the sinking feeling that I should have said something earlier. Who knows? Maybe backing out so late might even make me seem disloyal to the Cruise campaign?

On Friday night I hardly recognized the gym. The Dance Committee had transformed it. There was a blizzard of red and white streamers, a long refreshment table that held glass bowls of scarlet-colored fruit punch, and all kinds of snacks, from chips to little sandwiches. Red balloons and pom-poms decorated the table. On the bandstand, Winport Middle School's favorite group, The Bandits, was tuning up.

Gail Trent, the committee chairperson, beamed with pride. Everyone oohed and aahed as they walked into the gym. "Way to go, Gail!" Marcia yelled. Marcia laughed as she twirled around to show off the flowered dress that her mother had made for her.

Every eye in the gym was on the Cruise crowd when they walked in late. *Not only did they arrive like movie stars in their limo*, I thought, *but when they stepped through the doors, they all looked like they came right off of a movie set.* The girls wore dresses that were daring and expensive, and the guys were decked out in formal tuxes. Tracey's long, blond mane was held in place with a rhinestone clip, and the bows in Nicole's dark hair matched her pink dress.

Marcia was talking with Brian Reynolds by the stage when the crowd joined me at the refreshment table. "Hi, Lori," greeted Nicole with a dazzling smile. "Why didn't you come with us? You missed the limo ride."

"Yeah, Lori, you really missed out," said Tracey. "The backseat had a stereo, a VCR, a bar...everything but a shower! I felt like a star." She giggled loudly.

"We wished you had come with us," David pressed. "It would have looked good for my campaign if we had all arrived together."

Suddenly Marcia broke away from Brian and came toward me. I could tell by her face that she'd heard the whole thing. "David, when I promised to come with you guys, I'd forgotten my plans with Marcia. And when she reminded me last week..."

"Last week? Lori, you called me exactly one hour ago to tell me that you weren't coming. Why did you wait so long?"

"He has a point, Lori," challenged Marcia, her arms folded across her chest. "If you wanted to go with someone else, you should have said so." Marcia was smiling. Her voice was cool, but I knew she was angry.

"Well, I..."

Nicole looked at Marcia and then back at me. "I'm sorry if I said something wrong. I didn't mean to start anything," she said. "David didn't tell us why you changed your mind."

"Say, here's Marcia the ghost-buster, the girl who almost caught the big, bad Wolfman," broke in Bobby Troup, who'd been joking with Ms. Bosco and the other chaperons. "I heard the story yesterday from Pauline Beazer in health class. You're a really brave girl, you know."

Marcia's grim smile turned into a proud grin. "Well, you're exaggerating, Bobby. I only followed The Wolfman, I didn't try to catch him. Besides, it was Lori's idea. We did it together."

The crowd gathered eagerly around Marcia to hear the story. I backed off to give her the spotlight. In a way, I was grateful to Bobby for bringing up the Wolfman incident. Marcia was just beaming, flattered to be noticed by the popular group. I hoped she would forgive me for forgetting our plans to attend the dance together. I also hoped she wouldn't get carried away and mention Cap. I didn't want his name to be linked with The Wolfman. Bobby and plenty of other people had already spread enough rumors.

I munched on a chocolate brownie until the crowd around Marcia left. Just then, The Bandits began their first song. "Have we ever danced together, Lori?" David asked. "How would it look if the presidential candidate and his manager didn't get out on the dance floor together?" he asked.

My heart skipped a beat. I had to smile. "Yeah, it's about time we danced," I said nervously.

My eyes flickered down his handsome figure. David's blue shirt matched the color of his eyes. His loose, pleated slacks were the latest style. He'd never looked cuter. My heart hammered crazily as he led me to the floor, but I didn't mind the blood pounding in my ears. I was used to it. After all, it happened every time I was near David.

The song that played was slow, and it was one of my favorites. David put his arms around me, and we began moving in time to the music. "Lori, can you believe that story about Cap Cameron and The Wolfman?" he asked.

Oh, Marcia, you told them! How could you? I thought in horror.

I didn't say anything.

"Bobby swears he saw them together one night near the sea wall. Of course, he didn't get a really good look."

"It's so dark down there," I interrupted, realizing that it was Bobby who said that Cap was with The Wolfman. "Bobby couldn't be positive about who he saw, could he?"

"No, I guess not, but you have to admit that it's pretty weird." I was relieved that Marcia had kept her word and not mentioned Cap. I was becoming uneasy, though. One way or another, Cap's visits with Dr. Fisher were bound to come out. I wanted to protect him.

Over David's shoulder, I saw Cap and Eddie Waters entering the gym. They looked nice in their sports jackets and neat cords.

"May I cut in, Lori?" Tracey asked sweetly before the song ended.

No, I thought, but what could I really say? So Tracey and David began dancing while I went to look for Marcia.

"Lori, over here!" someone called.

"Cap? Hi!"

"Want to dance, Lori? You're wearing that white dress again. I really like it," said Cap.

"Thanks. I'd love to dance when the next song starts. Gee, Cap, you look nice, too."

Cap seemed unusually self-conscious. "The sleeves on this sport coat are a little short," he said, tugging on the cuffs. "It's last year's model, I'm afraid. Without my army jacket, I'm lost."

"I've noticed," I grinned. "Where you go, it goes."

"You know it was my father's jacket. He wore it the whole time he was in Vietnam."

"Did he keep it as a souvenir?"

Cap touched one finger thoughtfully to his lips. "Well, a sad souvenir. Dad didn't talk much about the war. I guess it was too painful for him." I noticed that sad look beginning to creep over Cap's face.

"Hey, the music's starting again," I said, smiling and touching Cap on the forearm. We began to dance. He really was a good dancer. I looked up at his smiling face. His jacket did look nice on him. Big deal if the sleeves were a little short. I mean, Cap was Cap. He refused to be labeled. I liked that about him. He wasn't handsome like David, but Mom said he'd be a distinguished-looking man someday. I kept staring at him. Maybe Mom was right. Hmmm. I think she *was* right.

"What's the matter, Lori? Have I got mustard on my chin or something?" he joked as he wiped his face.

"Oh, sorry. I was just thinking," I said. I was a little embarrassed that he'd caught me staring at him.

"Oh," he said, looking a little puzzled. Then he said, "Lori, do you remember the day you forgot your gym bag, and I waited for you to come back for it?"

"I remember. But you never said why you were waiting for me."

"I was going to ask you to come with me to the dance," he said as he blushed a little and looked down.

"You mean a date?" I asked with surprise.

"That's right, but you were in a hurry to

get to the meeting. And then you joined that Cruise campaign."

"So that meant you couldn't ask me?" Suddenly I felt a little flattered by all his attention.

"Well, things got complicated after that."

I knew exactly what he was talking about. I thought of the changes in my friendship with Marcia.

After that, we must have danced to nine or ten songs. It seemed like the evening was flying by.

By nine-thirty, Ms. Bosco and most of the other female chaperons had had their turns dancing. Cameras flashed as the older chaperons giggled and posed with the boys. Around ten o'clock, The Bandits played their last number. I looked around for Cap, but he was off dancing with someone else. I thought I caught him looking over at me. Just then Eddie Waters asked me to dance the last song with him. I kept teasing him about the skirt he wore on Primary Tuesday. He really was a good sport, laughing at all my jokes about his legs.

I looked over and spied Marcia dancing with Brian. *Looks like he managed to tear himself away from his pocket calculator for one evening*, I thought to myself and smiled.

But when the lights came on to signal the end of the dance, I couldn't see them anywhere. I figured she might already have gone to the coatroom to get her coat, so I headed that way.

When I got there I saw Bobby Troup fingering a small white card, squinting at it. A smile was building on his face.

I was puzzled. "What have you got there, Bobby?" I asked as I brushed past, pretending to search for my coat.

"Just look what I found on the floor, right under Cameron's old army jacket. Lori, this is our candidate's ticket to victory." Smiling proudly, he handed me the card.

It was an appointment card, the kind you get from dentists and doctors. Only this wasn't from an ordinary doctor. It came from Dr. Samuel Fisher, Psychologist. The name written in the blank space marked "Patient" was David C.—David Cameron. Cap.

"This is...oh, no!" I gasped.

"Think of how damaging this might be," Bobby said. "I always knew Cameron was out to lunch. Don't you think the voters need to know it?"

"Bobby, we can't use this information against Cap," I said.

"Why not? All's fair in love and war, and

this campaign is definitely war." He snatched the incriminating card from my hand, and at that moment the Cruise crowd came laughing and chattering into the coatroom.

Bobby shoved the card under David's nose. "What would happen if the voters found out this, Dave?" he asked. I saw David's face go white. Maybe he agreed with me. Tracey reached for the card. Her eyes went wide as she passed the card to Nicole. Nicole just looked at me. She was biting her bottom lip, a guilty expression in her eyes. Tracey was screaming so loud I couldn't hear what David was saying. It sounded like, "Where did you find that?" or "We shouldn't do that." I hoped it was the latter.

Bobby took back the card and slipped it into David's shirt pocket. "For safekeeping," he said. He smiled at David, and David smiled back, shrugging a bit. That tiny, crumpled card meant his success and Cap's defeat. But if I was on the winning team, why did I feel so sick?

Eight

O VER the weekend, I tried to put the appointment-card incident out of my mind. On Saturday, Marcia and I took the subway into Boston to check out the shopping malls downtown. We tried on clothes at a trendy boutique called Lafayette Place. We sat on a bench in the Boston Commons, admiring the flower beds while we threw corn chips to the pigeons. Marcia chattered on about Brian, the dance, and The Wolfman, but I didn't say much. I couldn't talk about the appointment card to anyone, not even to Marcia. She'd probably say I should quit David's campaign if I couldn't stop him from using the card against Cap. And I knew she'd be right. But I wasn't ready to make such a big decision. I still kept hoping the Cruise campaigners would change their minds and keep quiet.

On Sunday, the skating rink opened for the season. Marcia and I went there and wobbled across the ice. We both kept falling down, laughing at how weak our ankles felt. Then we spotted some girls from our homeroom. I was relieved that none of them mentioned Cap and The Wolfman. By Sunday evening, I'd almost convinced myself that David, Bobby, and the rest of the gang had decided to keep quiet. On Monday morning, it was Marcia who alerted me that Cap's secret was out—in a big way. I was climbing the steps up to the school when she rushed up to me, breathless. "Lori, I just heard that Cap's seeing a shrink!"

I let out a deep sigh, my shoulders sagging. Now she knew. So the gang didn't keep quiet. "Marcia, I know all about Cap's shrink. He's The Wolfman."

"He's what?" Marcia asked, her eyes wide.

"Well, there was a sign on the door of the Sturgis place when I went to peek in the window. The man's name is Dr. Samuel Fisher. He's a psychologist."

"You knew The Wolfman was Cap's shrink, and you didn't tell me?" she asked angrily.

"Marcia, please. Don't you see what a rumor like this could do to Cap? I'm sorry I talked you into following me up to the Sturgis

mansion that night. We—that is, I—shouldn't
have been spying on Cap, but it didn't seem
wrong at the time. I just didn't think anyone
should know. I mean, when I discovered it,
I didn't feel right to know about it myself,"
I explained.

Marcia seemed to understand. "It wasn't
your fault, Lori. The whole scene was so
weird. I couldn't wait to tell everybody about
chasing The Wolfman. I even told Mr. Flack,
the custodian. But I swear I never mentioned
Cap's name."

"I know you didn't," I said. I was so disappointed in the whole gang. At this point,
I was even wondering about David. It felt
terrible not being able to trust people.

"Then who did?" asked Marcia.

"Listen, I'll tell you the whole story at
lunch. I have a feeling it's going to be a long
day."

Marcia's version of the rumor was only one
of several. At least her version was accurate.
By the time I got to the cafeteria, my head
was spinning with the crazy rumors I'd heard
all over the school. One boy swore that every
midnight he'd heard moans coming from the
mansion. Another wondered if the shrink
looked like Dr. Frankenstein. And Louie
Mello warned that if Cap wasn't careful, he'd

turn into a werewolf. Most kids didn't believe this stuff, but nobody knew the truth. Cap's reputation was really on the line.

"Sorry I'm late," said Marcia, plopping down beside me and unwrapping her sandwich. Her green eyes were glued to my face. "Okay, Lori, talk. If I don't find out what's going on, I'll go crazy."

So I told Marcia what happened in the coatroom after the dance. She agreed that there was nothing we could do to stop the rumors without further involving Cap. Right after school, I hurried to the bookshop and confessed the whole story to Mom. She was rearranging a shipment of new books on the shelf.

"I wanted to talk with you about this before," I said, feeling a little shy and leaning on the counter. "It was really upsetting me. I didn't mean to spy on Cap. Now, stupid rumors about ghosts, werewolves, and the shrink are everywhere."

Mom stopped and pulled up a chair. "You know, when kids came into the shop with those Wolfman stories, I had no idea who or what they were talking about," Mom said. "I know Dr. Fisher was recently appointed psychologist for the Winport School System. He's very kind. I think he and his wife are remodeling the old Sturgis place. You'd like them. They do things their own way, sort of like Cap."

"Mom," I hesitated. "Cap's not crazy, is he?" I asked.

"Certainly not, Lori. People visit psychologists for lots of reasons."

"Yeah, and Cap's father died last year in Los Angeles. He must still feel awful about that," I said thoughtfully.

"I'm sure he does, Lori. I'll bet he misses his friends in California, too," she replied. "That's a big change in someone's life. I talk to his mother at the Parents' Council meetings. She's mentioned that he baby-sits for the twins when she works late. Now that's a lot of responsibility for an eighth grader."

"Maybe Cap's having a rough time coping with all these changes in his life," I went on. "Do you think that's the reason he's seeing Dr. Fisher?"

"Possibly," said Mom, "but whatever the reason, it's a personal matter. David Cruise shouldn't use such private information against another candidate. In fact, no one should ever spread information like that around."

"Thanks Mom. Talking to you helped," I said. I was beginning to feel a little better.

"I'm glad you understand how important

this is, honey," Mom said, patting my hand. "I think you should go and tell Ms. Bosco immediately about all of this. She might know what to do. By the way, did you see Cap at all today?"

"Well, I didn't talk to him. He passed me a couple of times in the hall, but I don't think he saw me. I called to him once, but I guess he was too far away to hear." I hated to admit it, but he ignored me when I tried to talk to him in health class. I remembered how hurt he looked, and I felt terrible. I couldn't tell anyone—not even my mother—that he was blaming me.

Before the first bell rang the next morning, I told Ms. Bosco everything. She ordered me to stay after school, when she would meet with me, David, Bobby, Tracey, and Nicole. Except for Nicole, all of them were furious with me for talking to Ms. Bosco. Their attitude soon changed after hearing what she had to say.

"I'm shocked and disappointed in your campaign tactics," she said as we sat together in the principal's office. "Visits to any doctor, for any reason, are strictly personal. I want these Wolfman rumors stopped immediately. I thought it might be helpful for everyone to learn more about psychologists, so I've invited

Dr. Fisher to address the junior high at a special assembly on Wednesday. He'll discuss ways psychologists can help students cope at home and in the classroom. All of you will sit in the front row during his visit."

After Ms. Bosco dismissed us, we headed to the library. Under the watchful eye of the librarian, we huddled around one of the big oak tables. They all listened as I suggested ways to put the incident behind us and get on with the campaign. This time David studied my notes for his final speech very carefully. Even so, he was content to make very few changes. When the meeting ended, I was fairly sure the Cruise campaign could be put back on track.

The whole school was packed inside the auditorium on the day of Dr. Fisher's visit. Everyone wanted to see The Wolfman. With her eyes on us in the front row, Ms. Bosco made a brief introduction. Scattered applause greeted the doctor as he stood up and walked to the platform. He wore a white shirt, an argyle vest, and a bow tie. His big, shaggy dog was by his side.

"Good afternoon, everybody," he said, smiling and tugging on the dog's leash. "As you can see, I've brought the wolf with me."

Giggles, grins, and a few whoops from the

boys greeted the doctor's joking remark.

"This is Dan," he continued, patting the animal's head. "Far from being a wolf, he's a mixture of collie, shepherd, and who knows what else? My wife, a teacher, found him abandoned on the highway ten years ago. Lie down, boy. That's it," he commanded gently.

Marcia nudged me from behind. "With that beard and those twinkling eyes, he looks sort of like Santa Claus," she whispered.

"Shall we begin?" asked the doctor. "Young people, have you ever had a secret, maybe a thought or a feeling, that you were ashamed to share with anyone else? You couldn't even tell your parents, your teachers, your brothers, sisters, or friends? Raise your hands if you've *never* had such a secret." Not a single hand was in the air. "I can't raise my hand, either," Dr. Fisher confessed. "Like you, I've done or felt things that I thought I couldn't discuss with others. As a psychologist, I've been trained to help people express their feelings more openly. Good communication is the first step toward solving problems at home or at school."

Dr. Fisher held our attention for his entire speech. After his address, he answered many of our questions. He warned that alcohol or drug abuse, divorce, or family illness could seriously affect school performance. He told us about many helpful services that his office provides, like special tests for hidden learning disabilities. He urged us to talk with our parents, teachers, or guidance counselor if we need help with any personal problems. Before leaving the stage, Dr. Fisher thanked us for inviting him to speak. "Remember, your teachers and I are your friends. We want you to enjoy your school years and to grow up to be healthy, responsible adults." He stood, giving Dan's leash a tug. "Come on, old boy. It's time we went home."

I joined the crowd of kids leaving the auditorium behind Dr. Fisher. I waved to Cap, who was sitting alone in the far corner. I know he saw me, but he didn't wave back. I was sure Dr. Fisher's talk would do a lot to help, but I still felt a pang of sadness as I looked at Cap's emotionless expression.

Nine

THE next morning, there was little talk of Cap's connection to The Wolfman. But everyone did talk about how much we liked the speech, and how we thought it would be easy to talk to Dr. Fisher. I certainly was glad that I talked to my mom. Otherwise I would never have had the courage to open up to Ms. Bosco.

That afternoon, I'd hoped that the Cruise crowd would agree to use the library again for our final strategy meeting on Friday. David persuaded everyone to meet at his penthouse instead. I didn't argue. David lived on the top floor at Harbor Point, the new condominium complex towering over the eastern end of Winport Beach. I was almost as curious to see David's home at Harbor Point as I'd been to see Rainesworth.

A lot of Winport citizens, including my

family, had opposed the construction of Harbor Point. They protested that a building that's 15 stories high would block part of the harbor view and cut off one entrance to the public beach. But the building went up anyway. The Cruise family was among the first to move in.

I rode my bike past the swimming pool, tennis courts, and vast underground garage. I locked my bike to a stop sign, entered the elegant lobby, and took the elevator up to the penthouse. Mr. Cruise met me at the door. "Well, well, if it isn't Lori," he greeted in a loud, hearty voice. "I hear David's campaign is going very well. Along with your strategies, I'll bet those posters I printed are doing the job, eh?"

"I'm sure they helped a lot, and, um, there certainly are a lot of them, Mr. Cruise."

"Good, good. I'm always glad to lend a hand," he responded, although I don't think he heard what I said. "The gang's in the family room. I'll show you."

I followed Mr. Cruise across the L-shaped living room. It had beautiful modern furniture and carpeting that was all color-coordinated in blue and white. I took a quick look at the dizzying view of Winport Beach and the Boston skyline before turning the corner to go into the family room.

I heard music. Mr. Cruise opened two double doors that were among several others in the long, paneled hallway. Inside, the gang was gathered around a wide-screen television as big as Tracey's.

"Got everything you need, kids? Lori's here!" he called out, smiling. Mr. Cruise was always nice to me, but he always seemed a little distracted. "Enjoy yourselves, gang."

David's family room was twice as big as ours. It had glass doors opening onto a balcony that ran the entire length of the penthouse. When Bobby saw me, he switched off the movie David had just rented. David looked over at me, then over at Bobby. They both looked a little nervous. Tracey and Nicole looked a little funny, too. The two of them were sitting near the window, and they stayed quiet. Bobby spoke up. "Um, Lori, we just wanted to say that we're sorry this whole thing with Cap got out of hand, okay?"

I was surprised, but very relieved. "Yes, okay," I said, not knowing what else to say.

Bobby continued, "Can we just get on with the campaign again?" David looked over at me. I could tell he wanted to apologize, but he didn't say anything. "Yes, let's do that," David said. I nodded and smiled. Everyone stayed quiet, so I dug out my campaign literature. Nicole and Tracey agreed to hand it out in the cafeteria during lunch on Monday. David skimmed the flyer we planned to photocopy and distribute. He did the same for my final copy of his major campaign speech. His mother, a slender woman who always seemed a little shy or nervous, brought us a tray of all kinds of goodies. After we quickly ran through the plans, David switched the movie back on, leaving my speech papers laying on the carpeted floor. I was just glad the whole thing was almost behind us. There was still one very important thing left to do. I had to talk to Cap.

Saturday was one of those rare, warm October days that make everyone remember summer and forget that winter is on the way. Marcia was visiting her aunt on Cape Cod. At about eleven o'clock, David called to invite me to a party on the Rainesworth patio that afternoon. I wanted to spend some time on the beach first, so he agreed to have his father pick me up on Seawall Drive at one o'clock.

I walked down to Winport Beach wearing shorts and a T-shirt. Some people were sitting on the sea wall, and some were lying on blankets on the sand. A few people were even swimming in the water. I stopped and rested on the cement wall, gazing out at the familiar Boston skyline and distant harbor islands. Gulls sailed across the cloudless, blue sky. It was a beautiful, perfect afternoon.

There was a boy sitting motionless at the water's edge. His back was to me, his eyes on the horizon. I realized that it was Cap.

An uncomfortable churning sensation began in the pit of my stomach. Cap had hardly spoken to me since the night of the dance. I didn't know what to do about it. Cap blamed me as much as David and the others for the appointment-card incident. Maybe he had a right to feel that way. Ms. Bosco must have talked with him about it, but I didn't know what she'd said.

I kicked off my sandals, and I crossed the warm sand to where Cap sat, cross-legged and staring at the calm, blue sea. I took a deep breath. "Hi, Cap," I said, trying to sound matter-of-fact. "What's up?"

"Not the surf. That's for sure," he replied after a long pause. He looked up at me, his eyes hidden behind a pair of funky sunglasses with bright yellow frames—pure Cap.

"Nice shades," I commented. "I've never seen sunglasses like those."

"I got 'em in Los Angeles, before we moved

here," he said, turning back to the view.

"I guess you miss California, huh?"

More silence. "Sometimes. Well, most of the time," he said, shrugging his shoulders. He turned to look at me.

Finally, we were communicating. I dropped down on the sand beside him, hugging my knees. "Aside from the palm trees, what's so different about California?" I asked, trying to keep the conversation going.

"Nothing. Everything. It's sort of hard to describe. In L.A., I'd sit on the beach like this almost every night, all year round. I'd wait for the sun to set over the Pacific Ocean. Here, you have to get up at dawn to watch the sun rise over the ocean if you want the same effect. You understand how it works?"

"The sun rises in the east, and it sets in the west. Sure, I know. So what else is different?"

He picked up a pebble that had been worn smooth by the waves lapping onto the shore. "Do you really care about this, Lori?" he asked.

"I do, Cap, honestly. Tell me more. What was your school like?"

"Oh, lots of people in L.A. are in show business, or they wish they were. Mar Vista Junior High had a great drama club. We did two shows a year. There were workshops in between, too. That's where actors get together and read plays or perform for small groups."

"I think they do that at Winport High," I said, trying to encourage him.

"That's good. You learn a lot that way. I'll bet Winport High doesn't produce a music video every year, though."

"Your school made videos?" I asked, surprised.

"No, they were Mar Vista High projects. I'd have gone there next year if we hadn't moved to Boston. Acting is important to me, but not as many people are into it here as in California."

"But, Cap, you were hilarious in the school musical last March! Didn't you hear? Mr. Cassidy is announcing auditions for another show right after Christmas."

"I liked doing the musical, but it just isn't the same." He tossed the pebble into the water. "What about you? What are your plans for the future?"

"I'm not sure, Cap," I said.

"No career in politics?" he teased.

If he was trying to annoy me, I refused to take the bait. "I do enjoy politics," I admitted. "My mother's race for school board first got me involved. Now, it's our eighth-grade election campaign. Maybe I will stick with politics as a career."

"You should. You're good at it," Cap said. "Why not try out for the debating club at Winport High? Debating teaches you how to discuss all sides of an issue."

"And you do it in front of an audience," I added.

Cap nodded. "You can't be a politician if you're afraid to speak in public," he agreed. "Lori, this may be none of my business, but aren't you a little bit sorry you didn't run for treasurer?"

"Sometimes," I replied slowly, stretching my legs out onto the golden sand. "Marcia was going to be my campaign manager. Maybe the two of us could have beaten Kelly O'Neill. Now, I'll never know."

"Has joining the Cruise crowd been as exciting as you thought it would be?" Cap asked in a quiet, serious voice.

I didn't answer. I took a good look at Cap. The breeze was tugging his shiny, brown hair back from his forehead. I smiled to myself at his wild sunglasses and Mickey Mouse shirt. He had every right to be disgusted with me, but he still took the time to give me good advice about my future. I used to think that

Cap was homely, but not anymore.

A car horn blared from the street behind us. Cap looked back. "It looks like Cruise's Mercedes," he said.

"What? Oh, that's right. David's picking me up here," I said, scrambling to my feet. "I have to go now, Cap."

"You'd better hurry," he said. "You don't want to be seen with a freak like me. Isn't that what your friends call me?"

"Cap, how can you say a thing like that!" I replied, a bit irritated. "I never called you a freak! I wasn't responsible for the appointment-card thing, either. I tried to stop them from telling, Cap, I swear. When things got out of hand, I went straight to Ms. Bosco."

"Am I supposed to be impressed? Your conscience may be clear, but you're still managing the Cruise campaign. Do you honestly think that David is the best choice for class president? Or are you on his side so you can ride around in his father's fancy car and hang out at Rainesworth?"

I felt numb with shock and anger, but it wasn't Cap I was angry with. All he'd done was put into words the questions I'd been afraid to ask myself. The horn blew again. "I'm sorry, Cap, they're waiting for me."

He removed his sunglasses and looked at

me. "It's your choice, Lori," he said.

"Cap, I'm sorry." All I could do was shake my head and walk away. I trudged back across the sand to the silver Mercedes that was gleaming in the sun. "It's your choice. Your choice. Your choice." Cap's parting words rang in my ears all afternoon on the sunny Rainesworth patio. Neither the laughter of Tracey's friends nor the blast of her stereo could drown out Cap's words.

After the party, David took us out for supper. There were long lines at the counter. David told us to order anything we liked. He wanted chicken nuggets and a hot apple pie. Bobby had the same. I asked for a hamburger, fries, and a chocolate shake. Everything looked and smelled delicious, but I kind of lost my appetite when David opened his wallet to pay for the food.

Stuck in one of the tiny leather pockets was Cap's appointment card.

The place was so crowded that we couldn't all sit together. Nicole Rossi and I wedged ourselves in with an older couple. The others were three tables away, huddled beside some kids from the high school. "Aren't you going to eat?" Nicole asked, munching on a french fry. "Your burger's getting cold."

"I really dived into those munchies at the

party," I explained, taking a bite of the sandwich.

"I didn't see you eat much at Tracey's," Nicole said. "You were definitely not in a party mood. Come to think of it, you've been that way since the night of the dance."

"I guess I have a lot on my mind," I said.

Nicole gave me an uneasy look. "That business with Cap's appointment card is still bothering you, isn't it?"

"Well, yeah, Nicole. It was nice to get an apology, but I happened to run into Cap this morning. He still blames me. He's still hurt. It was terrible. I still have to work it out with him."

She dropped the bag of fries onto her tray. She looked thoughtful. "I know spreading that story about Cap's shrink was wrong, Lori. I hated the idea, but Davey and the rest were sure it would force Cap out of the race. Especially Bobby. He'll do anything for David."

"I'll say. Bobby dresses like David, cuts his hair like David, and even orders the same food as David."

A sad smile appeared on Nicole's pretty face. "Bobby's loud and full of jokes, but he really doesn't have much confidence in himself. I think that copying David makes him feel like a winner."

"David did do a good job on the Olympics, and he's a top athlete, too," Nicole continued. "Still, his best fund-raising ideas came from Bobby. And Bobby never got much credit for them."

"I didn't know that," I said, looking at Tracey, David, and Bobby laughing together at the far table.

"Lori, please don't tell anyone about this conversation. It's hard to talk against my best friends, but I thought you should know the facts."

"I won't say a word, Nicole. And thanks." I turned down a chance to ride home with David. I wanted some time alone to think. Slowly, I wandered toward the beach, stopping at the sea wall where I'd noticed Cap earlier. I shivered in my thin T-shirt. The beach was deserted, and the breeze had turned chilly.

I remembered that at the start of the election campaign, Cap had asked me if I thought David was the best choice for class president. I was so thrilled about joining the Cruise crowd that I'd refused to answer. He asked me the same question today, and I still didn't answer. It was Nicole who set me straight. Okay, so my heart skipped a beat whenever David was near. That didn't mean I respected him. He used people. Last year, he stole Bobby's fund-raising ideas. This year, he had me writing campaign speeches that he was too lazy to write himself. David wanted to win, but I don't think he really cared how he did it.

Mom was right when she said the Cruise crowd wasn't much different from the rest of us. They might have more money, but they weren't always the most fun. In fact, I realized I was bored with Rainesworth. And I resented the fact that Marcia wasn't welcome there. After the election, I'd make it up to Marcia for the way I'd neglected her.

It was too late to quit the Cruise campaign. Cap had made big gains, but according to our latest poll, David was ahead by a large margin. The final speeches would be given on Monday afternoon, and the voting was set for Tuesday.

The term "heavy heart" seemed to say it perfectly. It was difficult to be excited about Tuesday. Wrapping my arms around myself to ward off the cold, I set off on the last two blocks of my walk home.

And things didn't get any better. On Sunday evening, I was slicing carrots for the stew we were having for dinner when Dad came in the back door lugging his golf bag. "Hi, Tom," Mom said as she rinsed a potato under the kitchen faucet. "How'd your game go? Dinner will be ready soon."

"Lori, the Camerons live on the corner of Main Street and Shore Avenue, don't they?"

"Yes, Dad, they do. Why?"

"Well, I'm not sure what's going on, but I just drove by there and saw an ambulance outside their place."

Ten

I grabbed my denim jacket and ran out of the house. I'd been to Cap's house only once, to work on his Captain Hook costume, but I knew a shortcut. When I reached Shore Avenue, I saw the red lights of the ambulance flashing in the darkness. Uniformed paramedics were carrying a stretcher into the Cameron's shabby cottage. A moment later, Cap came out onto the porch.

"Cap, what happened?" I gasped, trying to catch my breath.

He walked down the steps toward me, tears glistening on his cheeks. "Cap, what is it? Is it your grandmother?"

"No, it's Jeff," he sobbed, not trying to hide his fear. "Jeff sleeps with a special monitor in case he stops breathing. The warning buzzer went off. Jeff's face had turned this awful shade of blue. Mom was

107

shaking him, screaming for help, trying to switch on the oxygen unit..."

"How is he now?" I asked, my eyes on the lighted doorway.

"I don't know. The paramedics told me to wait outside. After I called them I telephoned his pediatrician at Children's Hospital. All I got was her answering service."

I took Cap's hand in both of mine. It was ice cold. "The doctor will call right back. Don't worry," I said, trying to soothe him and hoping I was right.

Cap's grandmother came out, holding Billy. The paramedics followed with Jeff's tiny form on the stretcher. He was wrapped in a fuzzy, blue blanket, and his face was hidden by an oxygen mask.

"Mom!" Cap called out, running to the woman leaning over the stretcher. They exchanged a few words. Like her son, Mrs. Cameron was tall and slim, with shiny, brown hair. She was trying to be brave. I could tell by the stiff way she stood, her head held high. The revolving red light on top of the ambulance swept the scene every few seconds in a blood-red glare. Garbled talk from its two-way radio droned in the background.

My mother's Toyota pulled up with Dad at the wheel. He killed the engine, switched off the headlights, and jumped out. I was glad to see him. I felt so helpless. Maybe Dad could do something positive for the Camerons.

I told him what happened. Cap's mother, a handkerchief pressed to her cheek, climbed into the ambulance behind the paramedic and closed the doors. With the siren screaming, the vehicle sped on its way into the city. Cap stood watching, his shirttails flapping in the wind, until the ambulance turned the corner onto Main Street and disappeared. "Are you okay?" Dad asked, touching his hand on Cap's shoulder. Cap looked at my father. His face was pale and expressionless.

"Cap, this is my father, Tom Stanton," I said.

"Oh, hi," Cap replied through his trembling lips.

"Hi, Cap. I wish we could be meeting under better circumstances," Dad said. "I've heard good things about you. Now, why don't you tell me how Lori and I can help."

"Thanks, but I have to stay here to watch Billy. I'm all right. I'm just worried about my mom. Jeff's doctor was waiting to operate on him until he was 18 months old, but he can't wait." He spread his arms in a hopeless gesture. "I hate the idea of Mom waiting alone all night at the hospital, but we don't have a car. There's no way for me to get there."

"Cap, can your grandmother manage Billy?" I asked.

"Sure, I guess so."

"Cap, why don't you get your coat, and I'll drive you to Children's Hospital," Dad suggested.

Cap descended the porch steps, pausing for a quick talk with his grandmother before putting on his army jacket. He joined us by the car. "Thanks a lot for the ride, Mr. Stanton," he said.

"Listen, you hang in there Cap," Dad said, opening the door. "I'm sure Jeff is going to get the best care."

"Yeah, I know you're right," Cap muttered. He turned and stared out the window.

The suburban traffic isn't bad on a Sunday night. In a few minutes, we joined the line of cars streaming into the Sumner Tunnel. Then we emerged onto the expressway that snaked through Boston's canyon of skyscrapers. "I like the city lights. Don't you, Cap?" I asked, trying to distract him.

"Yeah, sure. They're nice," he said. He looked over at me and forced a little smile.

I reached into my jacket pocket. "Hey,

want some M & Ms, Cap?"

"No thanks," he sighed.

"Go on, Cap. Take them for later. It might be a while before you get anything to eat."

"Okay, Lori. Thanks," he said, accepting the packet and stuffing it into his pocket. When he withdrew his hand, he was clutching a folded sheet of yellow paper. "Oh, my speech for tomorrow. I'd forgotten all about it," he explained. Slowly, he unfolded the paper, smoothing it out against his knee.

"Your speech? Can I see it?" I asked, a little hesitant.

"Why not? I won't be at school to deliver it, anyway." I took the paper from him and held it up to the window. I tried to make out the words in the glow from the lighted skyscrapers. "Hey, want to know a secret?" I asked, smiling. "Tracey and Nicole took our final campaign poll last week. Your numbers looked good. You haven't lost a point. In fact, you showed a gain."

"Maybe so, but my Thursday sessions with Dr. Sam killed my campaign, if I ever had a chance to begin with."

At that point, Dad broke in on our conversation. "We're on Storrow Drive now, Cap. Children's Hospital isn't far from here. We'll park and go inside with you to make sure you find your mother."

"Okay. Thanks, Mr. Stanton. Mom and I won't forget this. Hey, Lori, what's wrong? How come you've got such a strange look on your face?"

If I did, it was for a very good reason. The date on Cap's appointment card, October fifth, wasn't a Thursday. "Cap, is Thursday the only day you see the psychologist?"

"Yeah, Thursday afternoon or evening. Why?"

From the Cambridge bank of the Charles River, the lights of Harvard University formed wavy, golden reflections on the water. "I'll tell you why tomorrow, Cap," I replied, "after *I* deliver your speech at the assembly."

"Deliver my speech? But you're Cruise's campaign manager!"

"Not anymore. I just resigned."

Eleven

I hardly slept that night. I tossed and turned, worrying about Cap, little Jeff, and the confrontation I'd have with David Cruise in the morning. Hot cocoa, soft music from my clock radio, counting sheep—nothing helped.

Shortly after dawn, I gave up and threw open my closet. I tried on and rejected three outfits until I found the right one. It was going to be an important day. I'd be resigning from the Cruise campaign, explaining my actions to the class, and then giving my former opponent's speech.

I put on my new peach pants, a white blouse, and a matching blazer. I wore my black shoes that I'd been saving for a special occasion.

I called Marcia to tell her not to wait for me at the deli. She was stunned when I described everything that had happened the night before. She agreed not to discuss any of it at school until I had a chance to see Ms. Bosco. With Cap's speech tucked securely in my pocket, I gulped down a glass of milk and took off on my bike for Harbor Point.

Sailing up the long drive, I braked at the massive, brick entrance to the parking garage. I nervously paced the gravel as I waited for David. I had just about decided to enter the lobby of the condominium complex when David appeared. Luckily, he was alone.

"Hi, Lori. Nice outfit. I can see you're ready for our big day."

"David, I've got something important to say."

Some of the laid-back confidence left David's handsome face. "Sure, Lori. Shoot."

"David, I know you still have the appointment card that Bobby found on the coatroom floor. I want to see it."

Was that fear I saw in his big, blue eyes? "Aw, that old card? I threw it away."

"I saw it in your wallet on Saturday, when you paid for the food at the restaurant," I challenged.

He had no choice but to pull his wallet from his back pocket, flip it open, and slide out the card. He looked at it, gulped, and then he handed it over to me.

"David, the date on this card is October fifth, a Monday. That stuck in my mind because it's also my mom's birthday."

"So what?"

"Cap Cameron only sees Dr. Fisher on Thursdays. The patient's name on this card is David C. Tell me the truth. David C. is David Cruise, isn't he? *You're* one of Dr. Fisher's patients, too!"

"I...I..." sputtered David.

"Come on, David! Did you plant this card under Cap's army jacket for that sneak Bobby Troup to find?"

"No, Lori! I swear I didn't! My coat was hanging right beside Cap's, but he's such a kook that nobody suspected the card was really mine! I freaked when Bobby showed it to us."

"But you didn't have the guts to stop Bobby from using it to humiliate Cap. You tried to steal the election! Well, you can steal it without my help, because I'm not your campaign manager anymore. I quit!"

David looked crushed. "Lori, please don't tell anyone what you know! If my father finds out that I let people think the appointment card belonged to Cap, I don't know what he'll do! Dad hates cheating, but he wants me to be the smartest student, the best athlete, the most popular boy in school—he never lets up! I can't lose this election, Lori, I just can't!"

"David..."

Both of us spun around at the sound of Mr. Cruise's voice. The big man emerged from the dark garage entrance, his car keys dangling from his fingers. David went chalk white. If I weren't so mad, I'd have felt sorry for him.

"You two were shouting so loudly that I couldn't help overhearing," said Mr. Cruise in a quiet voice. "Young lady, why don't you go on to school now? I'll deal with my son."

I didn't think Mr. Cruise was capable of speaking so softly. He seemed like a different person. Mumbling a good-bye, I got back on my bike and pedaled to school. When I arrived, I chained it to the bike rack outside. I tore the appointment card to shreds and flung the pieces into the trash.

It was still early, and the corridors were quiet. I found Ms. Bosco in the guidance counselor's office, and we sat in one of the cubicles to talk. She already knew about Cap's baby brother.

After hearing the real story of the appointment card, she agreed that I should deliver Cap's speech to the class. She also suggested that I explain my reasons for resigning. "But there's no need to drag David's name through the mud," she said. "I'll talk with him after homeroom. Any apology to Cap or the class should come from David himself. Just tell the others that you and your candidate didn't agree on certain tactics or issues. Then mention the reason for Cap's absence, adding that in the interest of fair play, you've offered to read his speech. The kids will understand, you'll see."

During lunch, I telephoned Mom's bookstore for news of little Jeff. Mom hadn't heard anything yet. She said she'd call and let Ms. Bosco know the minute she heard anything. Marcia ran to Katie's Babies, a shop in Winport Center, to find a gift for Jeff. She bought a cute, kitten-shaped rattle.

Rumors and gossip filled the middle school halls, classrooms, gym, and cafeteria. Was the election still on? Where's Cap? What had Ms. Bosco said to David out in the hall?

Tracey and Nicole were friendly until they learned what happened between David and me that morning. Then Tracey shut me out as if I'd never been a part of the group. Nicole acted stunned. She didn't seem to know what to say. Bobby's rejection was more direct. "Traitor!" he hissed under his breath as he passed my locker. I just glared at him and slammed the door shut. I'd done what I thought was right. Bobby couldn't intimidate me. I wouldn't let him.

Like in the old days, "before Cruise," Marcia and I sat together at the election assembly. I was so tense I hardly heard any of the candidates give their speeches. Each one received polite applause and a few enthusiastic yells and hurrahs from their friends. Before I knew it, it was my turn.

I was trembling as I took the podium. Ms. Bosco must have realized it, because she made a special introduction. "People, as you probably know, a family emergency has prevented David Cameron from being with us today. Lori Stanton has an announcement to make, and then she will deliver the speech David wrote for this important assembly."

The auditorium buzzed with whispers. "Quiet, please," said Ms. Bosco. "I have one more comment to make, and I hope you'll listen carefully. Before marking their ballots tomorrow, wise voters will decide for themselves how they really feel about the candidates and the issues involved. Remember, the people you elect will have an effect on the future of our school." She looked over at me and gave me a warm smile. "Lori, would you like to begin now?"

Five minutes later, I sagged into my seat, dizzy with relief. Ms. Bosco introduced David. "Way to go, Lori!" Marcia whispered. "Cap couldn't have done better himself. You even got a laugh from that joke he threw in. What was it? 'I hope you all recognize me without the skirt?' That Cap!"

"Good thing I wore pants, or the line would have bombed," I grinned. Good old Marcia. And good old Cap.

David did a smooth job with the speech I wrote for him. I watched the audience, trying to read their reactions to my words.

Not once did David mention Cap's name or apologize for the appointment-card incident. But he did say something that really surprised me. "Many of us need help to deal with pressure at home or in school," he said. "If you're having a problem you can't handle alone, I hope you'll do what I do—visit the guidance counselor or Dr. Fisher, the school psychologist."

I expected gasps of astonishment from the audience. There were some, but David's confession drew a surprising amount of applause. And then it hit me. Trust David Cruise to find a way to turn the whole stinking mess to his advantage. I was so angry.

All I could think about was Cap. With everything he'd gone through and worked for, he deserved to win. I glanced at Marcia, my best friend in the world, and hot tears stung my eyes. Sacrificing my dream to run for treasurer had been foolish enough, not to mention the possibility of losing Marcia's friendship and Cap's respect, but the thought of watching Cap lose now was more than I could bear.

Twelve

JEFF was still in intensive care on Tuesday morning, but Mom said that was normal after such a serious operation. A very exhausted Cap arrived at school in time to shake a few hands in Ms. Bosco's packed classroom. Surrounded by his teammates sporting their campaign skirts, he was the last voter to cast his ballot.

Cap won the election by one vote.

Pandemonium broke loose as Marcia chalked the final count onto the blackboard in huge, round numbers. I got so carried away that I gave Cap a big kiss on the cheek. David Cruise edged away from his mob of disappointed supporters and headed in our direction. I braced myself for what might come next.

Without looking at me, he shook Cap's hand. "Congratulations, Cameron," he said.

"I concede the election. Good luck."

"Thanks, David. You know you're entitled to a recount. One vote? There might have been a mistake," Cap reminded his opponent.

"Forget it. I watched the ballot committee while they double-checked the count. I'm sure it was right on the money."

Eddie Waters grabbed Cap's hand, pumping it furiously. "Speech! Speech!" he yelled, dragging his friend to the front of the room.

David sighed deeply, his eyes focused somewhere in the middle of my forehead. He wanted to tell me something. I was feeling so good, I decided to help him do it. "I hope your father wasn't too tough on you yesterday," I said.

"As a matter of fact, he was. But for the first time since I was small, he listened to what I had to say. He said he didn't realize how much pressure he'd been putting on me. In fact, he called Dr. Fisher and made an appointment for the two of us to see him together. My mom's coming, too. Dad says it's time we got to know each other better as a family."

"David, I'm glad things are going better with your father," I said. And I meant it. I thought about how close I was to my parents.

"Thanks, Lori. In a weird way, maybe this

whole election campaign was lucky for me."

Lucky? I'll say it was, I thought, still feeling some resentment toward my former candidate. Losing meant he'd be able to avoid apologizing to Cap and the class for the appointment-card affair.

"Please simmer down, people!" called out Ms. Bosco. "First, the new class officers would like to thank you for your support. John, Kelly, Maria, and Cap, line up in front of my desk. Eddie wants to take a picture of us with the ballot committee for the school paper."

I moved toward the action up front. Tracey and Nicole shook hands with Cap, offering cool, but polite congratulations. I smiled at both of them. Tracey looked away, but Nicole smiled back, wiggling her fingers in a tiny wave. I liked Nicole. After everything that had happened, I hoped we could still be friends.

Bobby Troup was another story. Looking disappointed and angry, he watched the laughing winners line up for Eddie's camera.

Deception was Bobby's specialty, but he was smart. When he chose to be, he could be very diplomatic—even charming. After he calmed down, maybe I'd tell him how I felt. Bobby had too much going for him to live in another boy's shadow.

Cap's first, official duty as class president came a few days later. He went around to all the homerooms to invite everyone to the annual middle school Halloween party. This year's theme was "Famous Characters from Movies and TV." It was another one of Cap's great ideas, and everyone loved it. Marcia took the bull by the horns and asked Brian Reynolds to be her date. He accepted, and she's been grinning ever since. Their costumes are top secret, but I hear Brian likes old reruns of "Gilligan's Island." I kidded Marcia that she'd better start weaving that grass skirt.

I was on my way home from Sweet's Bakery on Saturday morning when I ran into Cap sitting on the sea wall. "Hey, Mr. President, how's Jeff?" I asked, hoisting myself up beside him on the concrete wall.

"Hi, Lori. Jeff's great. He's going to need a lot of special care after he comes home, but the doctor said he'll be fine by Thanksgiving. He was playing with the rattle you and Marcia sent over when I saw him yesterday afternoon. He keeps shaking it and smiling like crazy."

"That's because he knows he's coming home soon," I said, opening the bakery box. I handed Cap a big, chocolate-chip cookie, and took one for myself.

"Hey, thanks," he said, taking a bite.

"Listen, Cap, Mom let me in on an interesting bit of school board business. Ms. Bosco submitted your suggestion to use the Parents' Council money for a new computer. She also noted Gail and David's ideas for using those funds."

"You mean new equipment for the teams and sending the Vikettes to the championships?"

"Right. Anyway, a local computer company has offered to install a new system at a big discount. This means that with the funds the council raises this year, there'll be enough money to get the Vikettes to Springfield and replace at least some of the old sports equipment."

"Really? Now everybody'll be happy. That's great. Listen, Lori, I've got some news of my own. I volunteered to help Mr. Cassidy with the costumes for the next musical. He turned me down. He wants me to be assistant director instead!"

"Wow! You'll be doing him a favor. You've got more stage experience than anybody else at Winport. But aren't you taking on too many extracurricular activities? I mean, what about Billy and Jeff?"

"Well, this is the best part," he announced, edging a little closer to me. "The day manager at the air freight office where my mother works is leaving to go back to school. Mom's boss offered her the job. She won't have to work nights or weekends anymore. She'll be home by six, and she'll make more money. It'll cut back on my baby-sitting chores."

"What a break!" I said, giving him a playful shove. "Have you got your costume all worked out for the Halloween party?"

"Not yet. It's funny you should ask. I was hoping we could go to the party together."

A little flustered, I kept my eyes on the sand and sea. "Are you talking about a date, Cap Cameron?"

"You've got it. Maybe we could go as Romeo and Juliet," he paused and smiled, "or anybody else you want."

"Romeo and Juliet?" I echoed. "What a great idea!"

"I thought so, too. Think of the costumes. We'll do the cutting and sewing together, like we did with my Captain Hook costume."

"Cap, I'm warning you. I've never been on a date before," I giggled. "How about you?"

"Well," he said with a grin, "I'm not sure. Back in Los Angeles, I sat beside Kathy Lee Kirkmeyer on the bus during a class trip to

Disneyland. I bought her some ice cream. Does that count?"

"I doubt it, but tell me more about this Kathy Lee."

"There's nothing to tell. It was a short romance. We broke up in Fantasyland..."

I swatted Cap with my purse and exploded into giggles. Suddenly, the whole world seemed practically perfect.

About The Author

DEBORAH M. NIGRO was born in Boston, Massachusetts, and attended schools in England and New Zealand. After college, Deborah moved to Cape Cod, where she began working in a well-known bookstore. Among her customers were many famous people, including authors, and she became interested in writing.

Her stories and articles for children and adults have appeared in national publications. *Middle School Rumors* is her first novel written for young adults. Deborah also serves as a judge for the Romantic Writers of America "Golden Heart" competition.

She claims she reads anything she can get her hands on, including cereal boxes. Her favorite things, she says, are ice cream, cats, and almost anything Irish.